FROM THE HORSE'S MOUTH

ONE LUCKY MEMOIR

By Snoopy

As told to Gayle Carline

Published in the USA by Dancing Corgi Press

This is a work of fiction, based upon a true story. Some of the characters are fictional. Even the characters that truly exist have been modified to suit the author's needs. Unless you believe that horses really talk. Then it's all completely true.

Front and back cover photography by Lynne Glazer of Lynne Glazer Imagery (http://www.photo.lynnesite.com)

Cover art by Joe Felipe of Market Me
(http://www.marketme.us)

ISBN-10 0985506067
ISBN-13 978-0-9855060-6-3

ACKNOWLEDGMENTS

Writing as the human half of this book, I'd like to thank everyone who has helped me raise a very silly horse, whom I love very much even if he does want to bite or throw everything in his reach. My thanks to my trainers: Tina Duree Bevan, who steered me through his delivery and rode him to a championship in the PCQHA Trail Futurity, and Nicole (Niki) Owrey, who taught me how to be a better rider so I could forge a real working relationship with my big black goofball.

The doctors who saw Snoopy through his injuries also have my eternal gratitude. This includes his surgeon, Dr. Fischer, all of the staff at Chino Valley Equine Hospital (with a special shout-out to Dr. Klohnen), plus his regular vets, Dr. Kirk Pollard and Dr. Brigid Murphy, and the vets who gave me permission to push him through his rehabilitation, Dr. Martinelli and Dr. Rantanen.

Lastly, I'd like to thank my editor, Jennifer Silva Redmond, and my beta readers, Tameri Etherton, Ali Trotta, Sheri Fink, and Heather Gerard Barnes, who helped me strengthen the story with each comment and critique.

A NOTE ABOUT TERMINOLOGY

There is a term used when working a horse on a line from the ground. It is called "longe" and is pronounced "lunge." I was tempted to spell it the way it is pronounced, to keep non-horsey readers from stumbling over the term. But as soon as I did that, I knew I'd have all the horse people wailing that I don't really know what I'm talking about, if I could misspell such a common word.

So I thought I'd get it out in the open and hope that non-horsey people are happy to learn a new term and that the horse folk are confident in my knowledge.

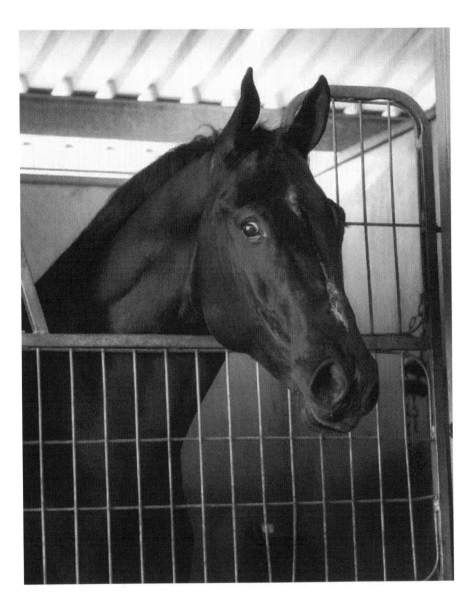

CHAPTER ONE

I don't know very much, but I do know what I am. I am a horse. Some humans say we aren't very smart. If that's so, it's not our fault. People train us, after all. They shouldn't teach us to be stupid.

I think maybe we are smart about some things. I know what humans are saying. Sometimes I can even feel what they are feeling, although not everyone and not all the time. Still, why can't they understand my language?

If I'm not smart, at least I'm lucky. I am eight years old now and I live in the same place where I was born. I am owned by the same woman who helped Mom deliver me—she still owns Mom. Her name is Gayle but I like to think of her as my MomToo. The ranch where I was born belongs to Miss Tina. She trains and rides me, along with Auntie Niki.

They are good trainers. I don't think they taught me to be stupid.

My regular name is Snoopy, but my big name is *My Flashy Investment*. Sometimes MomToo calls me by other names. When I step on her feet, she calls me Goober, or worse. I know what bad words sound like. When she gets me out of my stall and I grab my halter or my lead rope or her hands with my teeth, she calls me Bonehead.

Don't ask me why I do those things. First of all, if you don't speak horse, you'll never understand the answer. But mostly, don't ask because I don't know why. I just like to put my mouth on stuff. I like to feel things with my lips and my teeth. If I can throw it, I like to do that, too. I throw brushes and rakes. Once I tried to throw the stall cleaning man's bicycle. It didn't go very far, but he was still mad about it.

MomToo tries to make me stop grabbing things. So does Auntie Niki. They distract me or smack my nose, which makes me stop. For a little while. Then I forget.

As far as stepping on MomToo's feet, I guess I don't pay attention to where I walk, unless I'm going over poles. I'm very careful over those. It's fun to figure out which direction we're going and where to put my hooves so I don't hit the pole. Of course, it'd be more fun if I could ever pick a pole up and throw it. They're too heavy, though. I checked.

MomToo says I'm too full of myself. I don't know why that's a problem. What else would I be full of, except hay and I could never be too full of that. It's true, I'm a curious guy. Sometimes I see or hear something that gets me worked up, but I don't get afraid of much. I just get excited.

Maybe being raised on the same ranch where you were born and feeling like you'll never leave this place or these humans makes a young horse more confident about everything. There was never anything in my life that hurt me, until that spring day when I was four years old. That's when everything changed.

Of course, a lot happened before that day. I guess I'd better begin at the beginning.

CHAPTER TWO

I don't remember much about my birth, but when I was little, Mom used to tell me the story of the night I was born. I love Mom. She's so pretty. She is a bright, bright chestnut, but she has stripes of white hairs on her tummy, a blaze on her face and a big white spot on top of her tail.

Most of all, she has the most beautiful voice I ever heard. It's soft and low and she would let me snuggle against her every night while she whispered in my ear. She usually told me stories at night. I think she was afraid of the dark, but she never told me that. Instead, she would tell me a story.

"On the night you were born, the sun had just started going down on the most perfect of days. My Gayle came to the ranch early and got me out of the stall. She curried and brushed me and cleaned my hooves. She talked as she groomed me. I love to listen to her. I have listened to all her stories. That day, however, she was talking about me, how big I was and how slow I had become.

"It was true, I felt bigger than any draft horse. My belly was so full of you, I thought I might burst. Gayle walked me around the arena a few times. It was nice in the sunshine, even though I grew tired. She took me back to the barn, where our groom Hilde wrapped my tail so it would not get in the way in case I gave birth that day.

"I'll be honest with you, Son—I was frightened. You are my one and only baby and I knew you were large. I was afraid I would not be able to push you out. Horses usually have their babies alone, late at night. It is our tradition, from years of being wild. We leave the herd to quietly lie down and foal, then get the baby up and back to the herd as quickly as possible. If it's not safe to have our baby, we can even hold back the birth until the time is right.

"By early evening, Gayle was still at the ranch. Our trainer, Miss Tina was there, too. I heard Gayle ask Miss Tina if a horse's water breaks when they give birth. I realized this was my opportunity to have you while they were there to help. I relaxed and my water broke.

"Miss Tina laughed and said, 'It looks just like that.'"

This is where Mom would stop talking and lick my neck. Sometimes I was asleep by then. If I wasn't, I would ask, "What happened then?"

She would continue. "I could tell the first time I pushed, there was something wrong. You were stuck. I got up a couple of times and turned around, then lay down again, hoping you were rearranged. I love you, dear, but you were klutzy, even in the womb.

"Miss Tina saw my distress and stepped into the stall. She felt around inside me and found the problem. One of your hooves was folded back. You need both front feet pointed forward in order to slide out. She straightened your hoof, then helped me by pulling. I was already getting tired.

"At last, even Miss Tina was tired, so she told Gayle, 'Get in here and help out.' Gayle stepped in to the stall and took one of your legs. Miss Tina held the other. I pushed, they pulled and quick as a racehorse, you were out and cuddled up next to me, like you are now."

"And Gayle is my MomToo, right?" I'd ask each time.

"Right."

I loved hearing that story. Of course, I don't remember any of it as it happened. All I remember is opening my eyes, like I'd been asleep but couldn't remember the dream. I could feel Mom's warm body beside me and I could see MomToo in the doorway of the stall. She looked pretty blurry, but I think she was happy.

I heard a voice say, "You've got a colt." That turned out to be Miss Tina.

"He looks so dark," MomToo said. "What color do you think he'll be?"

They still ask that question. Sometimes I look very black. Sometimes I look dark brown. I have three white socks with freckles on my legs, and a star, a stripe, and a snip on my face. I know all this because I've heard MomToo describe me.

It's not like I own a mirror.

When I was born, a lot of humans came to see me. One girl said I had a lot of chrome. They all said I was flashy. I guess that's why MomToo named me My Flashy Investment. That's the name on my papers. I'm an American Quarter Horse. I know all this because Mom told me.

"You come from a very famous line of Quarter horses," she said. "Zippo Pine Bar is your great grandfather. He is in the Quarter Horse Hall of Fame. And your father is Artful Investment. He's an eight-time Superior Horse and was Reserve Super Horse at the AQHA World Show."

I used to ask Mom what my father was like, but she would just say he was tall, or quiet, or a big bay, or used other words that didn't really describe him. One day, I guess she got tired of me asking.

"The truth is I never actually knew your father. He lives on a ranch in Texas, which is a long way from here. They sent a silver box to our ranch and a doctor came and took something out of the box and put it inside my body and it made you. But I heard things about him from the humans who come here. They say he is a tall bay horse and quite a gentleman. I heard your MomToo say that was important to her."

After that, I stopped talking about my father. It would have been nice to know him, but it was okay. I know that MomToo loved Mom enough to look for a nice father for me.

I guess I should explain how I know about color. I've heard that humans think horses only see in black and white, but it's not true. We see lots of colors. We just don't care whether things have color or not and we only pay attention to the names of colors because humans do.

It's possible that we also see them differently than humans. MomToo does not even blink at a yellow bucket, but I can hardly look at it, it's so bright. She thinks my red blanket is shiny, but it looks dull and dark to me.

I've even learned about the names of colors humans use for us. Dark red is chestnut and light red is sorrel, brown with a black mane and tail is bay, and so forth. They sure have a lot of different ways to describe stuff.

So I could see Mom's shiny chestnut coat and look down to see my own white socks and freckles.

Me and my two moms.

CHAPTER THREE

When I was young, I spent every day in a big pen with Mom. It was on a hill and made of thick metal poles and wire that kept us from going anywhere else. The ground was hard. Across the path from our pen was a pasture. It wasn't big, but there were trees and some green stuff on the ground. It might have been grass or weeds, but it looked like it might be good to eat.

There were horses over there. Mostly, they wandered around the pasture. When it was hot out, I could see them on the hill, under the trees. Sometimes I watched them paw at the ground, then bite something. I didn't know what it was, but it sure made me wonder.

At the bottom of the hill I could see four white barns and three arenas, a round wood pen, and two human barns. When I pointed them out, Mom corrected me.

"Those are houses. Humans live in houses. Horses live in barns, in stalls."

Mom taught me a lot. For example, she taught me it wasn't nice to chew off half her tail hair. I didn't mean to do it, but once I started nibbling, I couldn't stop. Afterward, she chewed some of my tail hair and half of my mane, then told me, "See? Not very nice, is it?"

I already looked kind of weird, according to Mom. From what she described, my hair had started out black, then changed to brownish-gray, then it started rubbing off in patches. And my bottom was growing bigger than my front end.

Of course, I didn't care. I couldn't see me.

When I was a few months old, Hilde the groom came to our pen. He put a halter on Mom and led her out. I waited for her forever, but she didn't come back. I decided to call for her.

"Mom—where are you?"

I heard her call back to me right away. It sounded like she was down in one of the white barns. "I'm over in one of the stalls. Don't worry, we'll still see each other. And Hilde is going to bring a friend to keep you company."

She was right. Soon Hilde came back with one of the horses from the pasture. He was a grey horse, and not very tall, not even as tall as me. Hilde walked this horse into my pen, took off his halter, and left him there.

I greeted him right away. "I'm Snoopy."

"I have no doubt," he said. "You will call me Uncle Snowy."

The way he said it sounded like there was no choice. "Okay, Uncle Snowy. You are a very short horse. Why are you so short?"

"Because I'm not a horse, I'm a pony."

I thought about this. I knew I was a horse, because Mom told me. She said I looked like her. I had four legs with hooves, a mane and tail, a long neck, and two pointed ears on top of a long face. I trotted around Uncle Snowy, checking him out. He had the same things.

"So you'll never grow bigger?" I asked.

"Pfft, you know nothing, do you? I've got my work cut out for me."

"What work? And how do you cut it?" I reached forward to run my teeth across his hip—just for fun—but he kicked at me and trotted off.

"I am the teacher. I am put into pens with young horses to teach them how to behave."

"Oh. Mom said I was getting a friend to keep me company."

"Not exactly." He looked at me and laughed. "You look moth-eaten."

I didn't know what that meant. "What?"

"Like you've been chewed on by a flock of moths."

"No, just Mom."

Uncle Snowy rolled his eyes. "Well, at least you aren't raising a fuss. Some of the young ones I teach are such babies when they're taken from their moms. You only called after her once."

"Well, sure. I asked her where she was and she said she was in a stall and would see me soon."

"And you're built downhill," he added. "Your butt is enormous."

I looked at my behind. It was true, my butt was pretty big. "So what?"

"Well, I suppose it's a big enough engine that you could jump, but I don't know how anyone's going to ride you, and I hope your hind legs can carry all that extra weight."

I didn't know what he was talking about. "Ride me? What's that?"

"It's when humans get on our backs and tell us to go here and do that. When I was a young pony, they told me to gallop to a fence and jump over it. It was fun and I won a lot of ribbons. Now that I am older, I teach children how to ride, which is also a lot of fun." He turned and trotted away from me. "But it's something you don't need to worry about now. Built like that, you might never need to worry about it." I followed him and pushed at him with my nose, but he kicked me again.

Uncle Snowy taught me a lot of manners. I couldn't bump into him or nip at his butt like I did Mom.

"Get away from me," he'd say. "You can't run over everyone all the time. I'll tell you when you can come scratch my back."

I'd have to back away or he'd kick or bite me. His feet and teeth weren't big but they hurt. Sometimes he'd nod and I could scratch him, but I had to stand very still and scratch gently. If I bit or started chewing hair, I got a bite on my own bottom and a kick in my chest. Uncle Snowy was strict, but that was okay. I liked living with him.

CHAPTER FOUR

There were two goats in the pen next to us. They were girl goats, about half my size and brown, and had funny little tails that stuck straight up. I usually ignored them, since they were not very interesting. It's not like they ran around and played. They spent most days standing in the corner and eating, or looking for food to eat.

One night, I lay down to sleep and somehow woke up in their pen. There was a space underneath the metal bars just big enough for my body and I guess I scooted around to the other side while I dreamed. I don't really know how it happened, but I went to sleep in the pen with Uncle Snowy and woke up in the pen with the goats.

At first, they liked playing with me. They ran around the pen and I ran after them. Then they came over and sniffed my legs. That's when I saw their little tails wiggling.

I couldn't resist. I reached over and grabbed one goat's tail in my teeth and lifted. Her back end came off the ground, so I shook her up and down. She started yelling. I let her go and grabbed the other goat's tail. I shook her, too, then I dragged her up to the gate. She yelled even louder.

I dropped her and ran after the first one again. It was a fun game, chasing the goats and grabbing their tails. I couldn't quite throw them, but I could shake them up and down and drag them around the pen.

One of the ranch men came running. He caught me and took me back to Uncle Snowy's side of the pen.

He wasn't happy with me. Neither were the goats. Uncle Snowy wasn't thrilled, either.

"You are a doofus," he said. "Leave the goats alone."

"But it was fun."

"It wasn't fun for the goats." He shook his head, making his white mane wave in the hot sun. "Look, I'm a pony. I've lived my entire life being a pain in the butt. But I'm small, so they don't get that mad at me. I get cute points. You're six months old and already as big as me. No one will think you're cute when you're as big as a tractor, especially if you're pulling pranks."

I trotted a big circle around him. "But Uncle Snowy, fun is fun. Who cares about cute points?"

"You will when they whip you for being bad. Listen to me, Snoopy. The humans here are very nice. Some of the nicest humans I've lived with. They do everything they can to make us understand what they want. But if we misbehave, they spank us, sometimes with the whip. Just learn your lesson now. Leave the goats alone."

Even now, I don't know what everyone was so mad about. I still think it was fun.

CHAPTER FIVE

Across from me and Uncle Snowy, there were smaller pens. Holly was in one pen. She was a little gray mare, not much bigger than Uncle Snowy. Living next to her was Bonnie, a big chestnut and white paint horse. They were friendly, but spent most of their days with their noses pressed against the fence, sleeping or whispering together.

When I was still a yearling, MomToo came up the hill one afternoon. I thought she was coming to get me, but she took Holly out of her pen and led her down toward the barns. Holly was kind of an old horse and walked like every bone in her body was stuck together.

"She moves funny," I said.

"You will, too, if you live to be as old as her," Uncle Snowy told me.

"How old is old?"

"It depends. For horses, humans say we are old at twenty, but humans are still young when they are that age. You are a year old and huge. A one-year-old person is still carried around, unable to walk or talk."

MomToo came back leading Holly, who looked bright white in the sun.

I called out to her. "Holly, why are you so clean and shiny?"

"I am leaving tomorrow," she said. "I am going to the Clover Fields."

I had never heard of this place.

"But you are not as old as me," Bonnie said.

"No," Holly replied, "But you can still walk up and down this hill without much pain. My knees have been aching for a long time. Remember how Tina had to take me out of the pasture because the other horses were bullying me?"

"Yes. My hocks hurt, but at least I could stand my ground out there."

"Excuse me," I said. "But where are the Clover Fields?"

They all looked at me. Uncle Snowy tried to explain it.

"The Clover Fields aren't exactly a where, but a what. It is the place horses go when they die."

I had heard about dying and death from Mom, and sometimes saw birds and mice with no movement. Mom said everything had a *spirit* that was for always, but our bodies were only for right now. I didn't quite understand at the time. As Uncle Snowy explained, I tried to understand better.

"In the Clover Fields, we are whole again and may run without pain, and eat the sweet clover, and enjoy who we are. Others we have loved, humans or animals, can find us there. If we are needed, we can return to this place and allow our spirit to be born into a new body."

"Why would you want to leave a place like that?"

"To help someone we love."

I always believed what Mom and Uncle Snowy told me, but this was a lot to think about. Something bothered me.

"Holly, how do you know you're going tomorrow?"

"Your owner told me, while she was bathing me. She didn't quite get all the details correct. Humans don't know about the Clover Fields until they get there. But I understood what she was saying."

Her answer frightened me. "Is my MomToo going to kill you?"

"No, she just cleaned me up. It was sweet of her. She thought I should sparkle when I get to my destination. The doctor is coming in the morning. He will give me a shot that will make me sleep so deeply that I will be able to leave this body."

She hung her head. "I will miss you all, but I am looking forward to not hurting anymore. And I will have company on my journey, as Uno will be leaving, too."

Uno was a big red gelding. I had seen him around the ranch.

"Uno?" Now Uncle Snowy sounded surprised. "But he is younger still."

"Yes, but his front leg is giving out. I have heard them talking. The doctor has been out many times, taking pictures, and showing his heel sinking. He told his owner, Gayle, that she should not wait, or the bones would collapse through his foot."

"Gayle?" I cried out. "That's my MomToo."

"Do not think badly of your owner," Bonnie said. "Our humans love us and do not want us to be in any pain. Some pain we can survive and overcome. We heal. But Uno's foot will never feel good again. It is on its way from a little pain to a forever pain. Just as Holly's knees will never heal. Nor my hocks." She smiled a little as she spoke of herself.

"How do they know a sometime pain from a forever pain?" I asked.

Uncle Snowy scratched my withers. "They look you all over, they talk to doctors and take pictures of you, and they try everything to heal you first."

I remembered when I was little and my foot hurt when I walked on it. Every day, MomToo, Auntie Niki, and Hilde came to my pen and made me put my foot in hot water. Then Hilde would pick my foot up, dig around with the hoof pick, then put something black and icky on it and tape it. After forever, it stopped hurting.

Uncle Snowy was right. They tried everything, until I felt better.

We were quiet the rest of the day. Holly stood as usual, with her nose against Bonnie's at the fence. I thought about the Clover Fields and what that might be like. I didn't know what clover was, but Uncle Snowy said it was sweet. Apples are sweet, so I imagined a field of apples.

That wouldn't be too bad, but I'd have no friends there except Holly. Maybe Uno would be my friend.

I also thought about leaving that place to come back here in a new body. Did that mean my spirit was in another body before this one? It was hard to sleep that night. I couldn't imagine what I might have looked like, or why I couldn't remember a field full of apples.

It was early the next morning when Hilde came up for Holly. The air was cool, but I could feel the heat would be here soon. The ranch was quieter than I ever heard it before. None of us spoke until Holly was on her way down the hill.

"Take care," she called back to us. "I'll see you all again, one way or another."

As I watched her walking, I saw another horse at the bottom of the hill. I recognized him at once. It was Uno and MomToo was leading him into the big barn. I saw them come out the back. There were more humans there, but there were trees in my way and I couldn't see what was happening.

Suddenly, I heard Uno's deep voice. "Sorry about the bum leg."

I can't usually hear people when they are so far away, but I heard MomToo tell him, "Just find a new body and get back here."

After that, there was quiet, then I heard MomToo again. "Goodbye, Holly. I'll miss you."

A loud, rumbling noise made me look away. Something large with wheels on the ground and walls in the back rolled into the ranch.

"That's what the humans call the teal truck," Uncle Snowy said. "It will pick up the empty bodies and take them away."

"Where does it take them?"

"I don't know and I don't care. Holly and Uno don't live there anymore."

CHAPTER SIX

Uncle Snowy and I spent that winter together. When it wasn't raining, Hilde would come for me every day and take me down the hill. He would teach me all kinds of things and call me a good horse, then take me back to my home with Uncle Snowy.

In the spring, Hilde came into our pen. He put my halter on, and led me out. I thought we were going down the hill for one of my lessons. Instead, we walked across the path to the pasture and went in. He unbuckled my halter and let me go, then closed the pasture gate and left. I asked Uncle Snowy what was going on.

"You're too big to live with me, Snoopy. It's time for someone else to try to teach you a thing or two."

I was still confused. "How many things are there to learn?"

"A forever number," he told me.

That's when I went to live in the pasture with Johnny and Tucker. Johnny and Tucker were two guys who used to run fast and slide hard. At least that's what they told me.

"Turn and burn," Johnny would say.

He was chestnut brown, not as bright as Mom, but lighter, with a blaze on his face. One of his eyes was bigger than the other. Tucker was a bay with no white markings at all and a long, thick mane and tail. They weren't much taller than me, but they were really big guys, all stocky and hard looking.

"What are you going to teach me?" I asked.

"You'll see," Tucker said.

I knew what I wanted to learn first. "Why do I see you digging the ground and then eating?"

Johnny looked at Tucker and said, "Apples. There are apples growing under this ground. We dig them up and eat them."

MomToo had given me an apple before and I liked it. For the rest of the day, I went around the pasture and dug at the ground with my hoof. Finally they told me there were no underground apples. They had made it all up.

"Ha ha ha." Johnny laughed the loudest. "You're so gullible."

It wasn't the last time they made something up. Each time, they would laugh and call me gullible. I didn't know what that meant, but it made them happy, so it was okay.

"What's turn and burn?" I asked Johnny one day.

"They used to ride us in a big arena," he explained. "The man would make me run really fast, then slide to a stop. Then I'd turn around and run back the way I came, just as fast."

"Turn," Tucker said. "And burn."

That was the second time I had heard the word *ride*. "What's that mean, ride?"

Tucker described something called a saddle and bridle and how humans put them on you and expected you to carry them around on your back.

"Is it hard?"

"Not if they know what they're doing," Tucker told me. "If they can't stay balanced, it gets worrisome. Humans get upset when they fall off us."

"Yeah, they blame us if they can't stay on," Johnny said.

I thought they might be telling me something not true again, but I didn't mind. If it wasn't true, they'd call me gullible soon enough and laugh. I liked making everyone happy.

The one thing they both told me that I always believed was that if I ever tried to bite them or chew on their tails, they'd kick my teeth so hard I'd be pooping them out. They were both real friendly guys, but they looked big enough to do that.

I am growing up.

CHAPTER SEVEN

Even when I was staying with Uncle Snowy, or with Johnny and Tucker, my humans came every day and taught me things. Either Hilde or MomToo took me out of the pen and led me to the barn, where they brushed me and cleaned my hooves. Miss Tina talked about it being part of my training, but I don't know what I was being trained to do except stand still.

Before they taught me to be brushed and cleaned, they had to teach me to wear a halter and follow them on a lead rope. At first, I liked the halter and wanted to follow them around. Then, when I was four months old or so, I had a better idea.

Every time MomToo tried to put my nose in the halter, I would throw my head backward, then side to side and keep her from putting it on me. I thought this was a fun game. For about forever one week, we spent a long time wrestling with the halter. I thought we were having fun, even if her face was red and she looked kind of mad afterward.

Then one day, she put her arms around my neck and held the halter out in front of me. I was curious, so I pushed my nose forward. Suddenly I was haltered and our game was over.

MomToo was smart.

When Hilde the groom came for me, I never played the halter game with him. He was very gentle and spoke softly, almost like Mom, but you had to do what he wanted. I had to stand quietly for him to put the halter on, then walk behind him to the barn. I couldn't crowd him like I did MomToo. He was a firm leader and I could feel how strong he was when he told me not to do something. So I didn't do it.

Standing still was harder than it looked. At first, they made me stand still when they held my lead rope. Then Hilde started to walk me in and out of a place with hard ground and poles like the ones around my pen, only fatter. We would stop at the end, where the tall poles were, and I had to stand there. After forever, he hooked a chain on either side of my halter and I had to stand without him.

I learned these were called cross-ties and all the horses had to stand still in them. Once I found out I could chew on the chains, it wasn't so hard to do at all.

They say I get bored easy, but I don't think I get bored at all. The world is too interesting to get bored. I want to look at it all. And touch it with my teeth.

I also had to get used to having a bottle pointed at me and wet stuff sprayed on my body. It smelled funny. At first I used to curl up my lip because it smelled so funny. MomToo would say, "I know it smells bad, but it will keep the flies off you."

I don't know why flies are bad. That's why God made tails.

One day, I was practicing my standing still in the cross-ties, when MomToo walked by leading another horse. It was Mom. I was so excited I had to whinny a little bit.

She was not as excited. "Hello, Snoopy."

"I have been learning so much, Mom. See how I stand in the cross-ties without wiggling or backing up?"

"That's good. What else have you learned?"

"To be brushed and have my hooves cleaned, and to be splashed with water and sprayed with smelly stuff for flies." I chewed my chain and looked over at her. She was chewing her chain, too. I told her everything I had learned since she went to live in the stall, from *don't throw goats,* to *don't bite other horses.*

Holly's face appeared in my mind.

"I learned about the Clover Fields, too."

"Ah, yes. Holly and Uno. They are not the first I've said goodbye to. You were in the corral near her. Do you miss her?"

"Yes, a little. But she said she might come back if she was needed. So I've been looking for her."

I watched Mom being saddled and thought about what Uncle Snowy had told me.

"Mom, did I come back from the Clover Fields to help someone?"

She didn't answer at first. "To be honest, Snoopy, you are not a complex horse. I love you, but you are a simpleton. I do not believe you have an old spirit."

"So my spirit has never been used before in another body? It's brand new?"

"I can't say for certain. But it's not so bad to be brand new."

MomToo led her to the arena, cutting our talk short. I wasn't sure if there was more to say, anyway. I was not complex, in Mom's eyes. I was a simpleton, a new spirit. This gave me even more to think about.

How would I find my way to the Clover Fields if I'd never been there before?

CHAPTER EIGHT

I stood in the cross-ties until Hilde led me away on a long, long rope. We went to the round, wood pen. I liked the wood pen. The dirt was soft and you could run and play in it. But Hilde told me I couldn't play. He held onto the rope and let me walk away from him, then he picked up a big orange stick with a wiggly tail and waved it behind me. It made me want to go faster to get away from the wiggly tail.

We started doing this all the time. I learned the orange stick was called a whip and this was called longeing. I was supposed to walk, trot, and gallop on this long rope, then stop when Hilde said, "ho," and turn around to go the other direction.

It was pretty easy to learn, although sometimes I liked to pretend I didn't understand so I could keep running in one direction, jumping and bucking and playing. Hilde always stopped me and made me do it right.

This became our routine. I'd come down the hill with Hilde, get brushed and sprayed, then go to the wood pen and run back and forth.

I learned to stand in the hard place and have water sprayed all over me. Johnny told me this was called the wash rack. A few times there was a horse next to me and I tried to say hello by scratching them with my teeth, but Hilde always told me no.

Sometimes MomToo brought me down to brush and clean. Once or twice, she tried to longe me. I went around a few times, then wanted to play, so I started backing up and jumping and pulling instead of going forward.

After that, MomToo left my lessons to Hilde, which wasn't as much fun, but I learned a lot. He didn't let me play or mess around. He was never mean and never hurt me. He just told me to stay away from him and I did.

I got really good at longeing, so good I didn't have to be on the long rope. Soon, even MomToo could take me into the wood pen and I would stay at the edge and do what she said. If she made a clucking noise, I was supposed to trot. If she made kissing noises, I was supposed to gallop. If she said, "ho," I stopped.

It was fun, spending time with her and Hilde, then in the pasture with my friends.

During one lesson, Hilde brought extra toys into the wood pen. There was another long rope and a weird-looking belt that was short and thick. We stood in the middle of the pen together while he took the belt and rubbed it on me. It felt good. I reached around to grab it, but he pushed my face away.

Then he put it on my back. It still felt good. I couldn't figure out why he was doing this. Was it some kind of new game?

Then he tied the belt around my tummy and my back so it wouldn't come off. That tickled. When he let the long rope out for me to run, I started jumping and bucking because it tickled so much. After a while, I didn't notice it anymore and just ran like always. I ran until I was tired, which is when Hilde usually took me out.

But that day he didn't. Instead, he took my long rope and moved the clip to the buckle next to my nose. He attached the rope to the belt around my tummy. After that, he did the same thing to the other long rope he brought, clipping it to the other side.

I couldn't believe what happened next. Hilde walked behind me, holding both ropes. He pulled on one rope. At first I tried to yank my head the other way, but he kept pulling until I moved toward it, then the pulling stopped. Then he pulled on the other rope. Again, I shook my head up and down and away from the pull. Nothing worked until I went toward it. After a couple of times, I figured this game out and went wherever I felt the rope tug.

I couldn't wait to get back to the pasture and tell Johnny and Tucker about this. I was so excited, I was a big jumble of words trying to describe the belt around my tummy.

"Oh, that's a Sir Pringle," Johnny told me.

Tucker disagreed. "It's Sir Single."

"Maybe." Johnny nodded. "At any rate, you are learning to be ridden."

"But Hilde didn't get on my back like you said he would," I said.

My two friends looked at each other. "He will."

Johnny pulled at a piece of grass. "These humans are pretty gentle here. In some places, they tie you up, throw a saddle on your back, then some crazy man gets on you and kicks you until you understand he's in charge."

"Wow." I was hoping this was one of their jokes. It didn't sound like fun at all.

"Here, they put the Sir Single on you, so you get used to having something tied onto your back, under your belly. Next, they'll put a saddle pad under the Sir Single, then they'll trade the Sir Single for a saddle."

Tucker interrupted. "After a long time, they'll finally lay across the saddle, then step into the steer-up, spend half the day teaching you it's okay to have them on your back."

I had bunches of questions. "What's a saddle? What's a steer-up? What's a saddle pad?"

Johnny's eyes widened, even the little one, so I could see the whites. "Haven't you looked at that big mess of stuff in the barn? The flat things are pads. The lumpy brown things are saddles. The loops at the bottom of the saddles are steer-ups."

Although Hilde took me into the barn to brush me, I never thought much about the big stack of stuff in there. I looked at it a lot, but he never used any of it on me, and he never let me get close enough to taste it. If I couldn't taste it, I tried to ignore it.

I was going to have to take another look.

CHAPTER NINE

A week later, after working with Hilde and the Sir Single, he took me to a regular stall instead of taking me back to the pasture with Tucker and Johnny. I thought maybe I would only be there for a little while. Sometimes after they sprayed water on me, they let me stand in the sun until my hair dried. I waited to go back to the pasture, but no one came to take me home.

It was okay, though. The stall was made out of the same kind of poles as the pen where I stayed with Uncle Snowy, except I didn't have as much room. I did have two new neighbors on either side of me. They had pens of their own. I introduced myself to both of them.

"Hello. I'm Wendy." That was my neighbor on the right. She was brown and big, but not as big as me.

"Hi, Wendy, I'm two years old, almost three. How old are you?"

"Older than that, young man. Now, just keep to yourself and don't steal any of my food, and we'll get along fine." She turned her head to the corner of the stall and closed her eyes.

I turned to the neighbor on the left. He was a bright bay, a little taller than me, but skinnier.

"I'm Rusty," he said. "I'm three."

He was very busy in his stall, wandering around and banging on the metal with his hooves.

"Your feet sound really loud on the poles," I told him.

"I just got shoes. Look." He put his front foot on one of the poles and I could see a line of silver on the bottom and some funny marks on his hoof.

"That looks shiny. Did it hurt?"

"No, Silly. The man trimmed the bottom, then nailed them on, then smoothed everything down with a rough stick." He straightened his leg so that he was standing on the pole, then put his other front leg on the next higher one.

"Are you sure you should be climbing the stall?"

"Sure, I do it all the time." He moved the lower foot up to meet the other, stretched out tall until his head almost touched the roof, then pulled his feet down and bounced on all four legs. "How do you like to be ridden? English or Western?"

"I don't know. What's English and Western?"

Rusty laughed. "Western is a big heavy saddle and they make you go slow. English is a little saddle and they let you go faster. I like to go faster. Slow is boring." He did another turn in his stall and another jump.

"Do you always run around so much?"

"Sometimes. Maybe. Yeah, prolly." He twirled again. "But it's dinner time, so I feel like I can't stand still."

Rusty nodded toward the barn next to us and I saw the ranch man pushing a cart full of hay. The man was coming toward us, which made me excited.

I like dinner. In the pasture we got breakfast and dinner, but there were also clumps of stuff growing that we could eat whenever we wanted. So even though I liked hay a lot, I never had to rush to dinner, especially with Johnny and Tucker. They always ate first, anyway, and made me wait.

This time, the ranch man put a big flake of hay in my feeder. I leaned in and took a bite and no one else barged in to chase me away. It was all mine.

I missed Tucker and Johnny, but having my own hay in my own stall was good.

CHAPTER TEN

It turns out, Johnny and Tucker weren't teasing me about my training. One morning, Hilde brought something new into the wood pen. After listening to my friends, I took a look at the things in the barn. There were flat things and lumpy things, just like they said. Hilde had carried one of the flat things with him.

He showed it to me and let me sniff it. I wanted to pick it up and throw it—it looked like it would go a long way, but he wouldn't let me. Instead, he brushed it against my side, then my back. I tried to move away to get a better look at what he was doing, but he just kept close to me, rubbing me with the flat thing.

After a while I got used to the rubbing. It felt good. I still tried to grab it, but Hilde said no. Then he put it on my back and tied it there with the Sir Single.

Oh, it tickled my hips! I ran to the edge of the wood pen and jumped and galloped and bucked, trying to get it off. Soon it stopped tickling, so I stopped jumping and did as Hilde said. I galloped, then trotted, then galloped again, then walked. He turned me around and had me do the same thing in the other direction.

When I was very sweaty and tired, he put the other long rope on me and I walked around, my nose being pulled this way, then that. Just when I was happy to go right, he would tug on the left rope.

By now I had learned that tossing my head and fighting made the lesson last longer. If I did what he asked, we could be done and I could go back to my stall.

After forever we were done and I was taken to the wash rack to have water sprayed on me. I don't understand why they wanted to spray water on me, since I was already sweaty, but I was happy to stand still and try to play with the hose. If it was close to my foot I could step on it and make the water stop. If they offered me a drink I could grab the hose in my mouth and shake water on them. It was a great game.

After the wash rack I went to the Walk-Around machine. Auntie Niki called it a hot walker. It looked like a big metal tree with branches sticking out sideways but no leaves to eat. Hilde or Auntie Niki would clip me to one of the branches. Sometimes the tree trunk would make a growling noise and pull me forward so I walked around and around. Usually when I was wet, the tree didn't growl or pull me. I could stand and sleep in the sun until I was dry and Hilde led me back to my stall.

Rusty was waiting for me when I got back that day. He was a nice horse, even if he was busy doing something all the time. Wendy would complain about him a lot.

"Why don't you just settle?" she asked. "Why do you always have to be wandering around, climbing your stall?"

He'd laugh. "Why not? It's fun, right, Snoopy?"

I didn't really know if being so busy was fun, since I liked standing still in my stall and was never in the mood to climb up the metal poles. Wendy's idea was pretty good, that a horse should save their energy. Hilde made me pretty tired every time he gave me a lesson, so I was happy to rest afterward.

"Do not listen to him," Wendy told me. "He may be a year older than you, but he has always been too active for his own good. He was running circles around his mother when he was only a few hours old. Do you see how big he is? He will wear himself out before he is fifteen."

"Were you born at the ranch, too, Wendy?"

"No, I was born on another ranch, a long way from here. I wasn't even born in a stall, but out in the field late one night. My mother was part of a small herd. I grew up surrounded by other foals and mares."

She was a plain horse with no markings, but the hair on her flank grew in funny squiggles. "Why is your hair so funny there?" I asked her.

"That is a brand. Because different humans owned different horses in the herd, they marked us all so they could tell who owned which ones."

"Did it hurt?"

"A little. I was fairly young. The men who did it were efficient, if not very gentle about it. They led me into a small stall, just big enough for my body to fit into. I was nervous, but one of the men rubbed my neck and withers until I felt somewhat calmer. Then I felt a cold pressure on my flank that stung. It stayed for a few moments, then went away, and they turned me loose."

"I don't remember having that done." I looked at each side of my body. "I guess I don't have a brand."

"No, none of the horses born here have one." She walked over to her water dish and drank. "You have been coddled."

"What's *coddled*?"

"You are born in warm stalls on soft straw, surrounded by humans to help in case something goes wrong."

"You say that like any of us has a choice," Rusty said as he knocked his hoof against the metal.

"None of us has a choice," Wendy told him. "You simply received more attention than I did. You don't know what it's like to be pushed into the cold air, nuzzled into standing and forced to walk through the dark toward a group of fuzzy strangers. And I do not know the feeling of spending days, weeks, months in the sole company of my mother, without being on the constant move."

"I would have liked that," Rusty said. "I like to be on the move."

"I guess I would be happy either way," I told them. "Since I wouldn't know any difference."

"You're too easy going," Rusty told me. "Humans are going to expect you to do whatever they want."

"Well, why not?"

"Why should we? I mean, okay, some days I get along fine with my owner, and with Niki. But if I'm not in the mood to do something, I at least make them give me a good reason to do it."

"I just figure, if I do what they ask I get to finish and go back to my stall."

"That's smart," Wendy told me.

"That's stupid," Rusty said. "You're such a chump."

I suppose I should have been mad about being called a chump, but it was okay. Rusty's brain liked to go as fast as his body. I probably am too easygoing. I just never saw the point in fighting everyone, especially my humans. They were really strict, but they usually played good games.

CHAPTER ELEVEN

Once I got used to the flat thing, called a saddle pad, under my Sir Single, Hilde brought a lumpy thing to the wood pen. I recognized this was a saddle. He let me see it, but I couldn't touch it or chew it or throw it. Hilde didn't share this toy.

He put the saddle pad and the saddle on my back. It felt very heavy, so I stood still, hoping it would go away. It didn't, though. Instead, Hilde put a strap around my belly and tightened it so the saddle would stay on. Then he let out my long rope and picked up the whip.

Boy, did I buck and jump. The saddle bumped up and down on my hips, which really tickled and made me jump around more. Hilde held onto the rope and let me play, until I stopped bucking and started running. Then we went to work on my lesson, walking, trotting, galloping, in each direction.

Again, after I was tired and sweaty he put the two long ropes on my halter and walked behind me. He flapped the ropes against my sides and made a little clucking noise with his mouth to make me walk, then said, "Good boy," when I did. As usual, he pulled on one side of my halter and when I moved in that direction, he stopped pulling, with another "Good boy." Then he pulled on the other side. There was always a "Good boy" each time I did what he asked.

I thought about what Rusty said. Why wouldn't I want to do what humans tell me, when they say I'm a good boy?

We did this every day, until the day Johnny and Tucker had told me about. Hilde had saddled and longed me, then instead of putting two long ropes on me, he put two short ropes on my halter. Then we stood still for a long time. He kept pulling on one of the steer-ups, then rubbing my shoulder and calling me a good boy.

I didn't know what I was being so good about, but I was tired, so it was nice to stand still.

After a while, he put a box next to me and climbed on it. Then he laid his body on top of the saddle. He didn't tell me to do anything about this, so I didn't. Again, he told me I was a good boy. Next, he stood up and put his foot in the steer-up. I had this figured out by now. Standing still was good.

I stood still. I got another pat and another "Good boy."

After a long time of standing, Hilde stood in the steer-up again, then sat on my back. It felt a little different. He was much heavier than when he just laid across me. But I knew what to do. I stood still and collected my "Good boy."

Then I felt him tapping my sides and heard the clucking noise. Could he be asking me to move with all this weight on me? I stepped forward, one step, and heard "Good boy." I took another step, and another, each time hearing I was a good boy to do it.

Slowly, I walked around the wood pen, Hilde on my back, telling me I was good. Just like with the long ropes, he pulled one side of my halter with the lead rope, then he pulled the other. Each time, I turned into the pull and was rewarded. This wasn't so bad.

Afterward, I got a nice long spray with the water. Hilde talked to me the whole time about what a good horse I was, that I was even better than my father. That's the first time I heard him talk about my father. I wished he could speak my language—I had a lot of questions. Instead I just listened.

Back in my stall, I had big news for Wendy and Rusty.

"I got ridden today for the first time."

"Weird, huh," Rusty said. "Did they use the heavy saddle?"

"I suppose so. It seemed heavy."

"Who rode you?" Wendy asked.

"Groom Hilde."

"I've never been ridden by him," she told me. "Was he any good at it?"

"Golly, I don't know. How can I tell?"

"A good rider stays in the middle of you so you don't feel like they're too heavy on one side. You can feel their seat pressing into your back in a firm and even way. Their legs and hands stay quiet and are only used when necessary, so there's not a lot of waving and flapping about."

I thought about her rules and Hilde on my back. "Yes, he was good at it."

"Hilde rode me first, too," Rusty said. "He was all right."

"Don't all humans ride us like that?"

Wendy laughed. "Not at all. I used to be ridden by good riders. Knew how to use their seat and legs and hands. They made me work, but it actually made my body feel better to have my hips pushing forward and my back rounded. Now I'm a lesson horse. I like teaching, but it gets tiresome sometimes. The riders lean forward and back and right and left, and pull on the reins to try to balance their bodies. Then they let their legs flop against my sides, which makes me speed up, then pull back on the reins because I'm going too fast. It's a good thing the trainers use a mild bit for my mouth. Otherwise, my lips would be sore from all the yanking about."

"Bit? What's that?" I asked

"It's a big metal stick they poke into your mouth," Rusty said.

Wendy laid her ears back at him, annoyed. "Don't frighten him." She turned to me. "In addition to a saddle, you will learn to have a *small* piece of metal in your mouth. It lies against your tongue and the corners of your lips, so it doesn't touch your teeth. Some horses like it because some metal tastes sweet, and they like to play with it in their mouths."

"Some bits are huge," Rusty added.

"Some bits are, but at least here, you are only asked to wear the bit that fits you and your rider. If one of the trainers uses a big bit on you, they will use it with care and will not hurt your mouth. If you have beginning riders, like me, they use a very soft bit that you can mostly ignore."

I thought about having something in my mouth. I like chewing on things and touching things, so I decided it would be all right. I guessed it would be kind of like when Hilde pulled on my halter. Instead, he'd pull on this bit-thing and I would move my head.

"I forgot," I said. "When I was being sprayed with water, Hilde told me he used to know my father."

"So?" Rusty asked.

"Well, I never met him and Mom said he was never here. But I guess he was, if Hilde knew him."

"Who's your father?"

"Artful Investment."

Rusty laughed. "He's my dad, too. Who's your mom?"

"Frostie. She lives here."

"Oh, my mom's Molly. She used to live here, but she got sold."

"Sorry."

Rusty climbed up a bar and stretched to the roof. "No problem. I barely remember her."

I watched him jump down and twirl around. So he was my half-brother. We were both tall, but he was skinnier than me. He also liked to move around more. He was a bay, like our dad, but maybe he was more like his mom in other ways.

Families are sure interesting.

CHAPTER TWELVE

For about forever, my days looked mostly the same. Hilde now put the saddle on my back when he was finished brushing me in the barn. I would run in the pen, he would ride me and then we would come back to get unsaddled, washed, and put back in the stall.

They were easy days.

From my stall, I could watch the other horses being ridden in the big arena. Rusty usually had Auntie Niki on his back, or sometimes his owner. He always looked like he wanted to go fast, but everyone kept telling him to slow down.

Wendy had different humans on her every time. Usually Auntie Niki or Miss Tina was on the ground, telling them to do things. Once, when Wendy was back in her stall I asked her what they were telling her to do.

"Oh, they're not talking to me, they're talking to the student. The human is learning to ride and they're giving them commands to make me stop or go, or turn or trot." She shook her head. "Of course, I understand what they're telling the student to do. If I think the student is sitting correctly and giving me the right cues, I obey. If not, then I try to teach them to do it right."

"How do you teach them?"

"I don't obey until they are correct. Especially when they're asking for a turn. If their weight is on the wrong side of my body, I don't turn when they pull the rein. I bend my middle, so my head is facing one direction and my shoulders are facing another."

"Wow, my riders never do that," Rusty said. "That might be a fun game."

Wendy shook her head at him. "It's not a game. Your riders are trained already. They are not going to lean the wrong way or yank on your mouth. You would have no excuse to misbehave."

"Don't they get mad at you?" I asked.

"Sometimes. They are definitely frustrated. I am sorry about that. But Tina and Niki know it is not my fault, so they work with the student to correct what they're doing wrong. At the end of the day, I know that I have done all I can do to help them understand me."

One day, Auntie Niki came to my stall and got me out. She brushed me and put on the saddle, then led me to the wood pen, holding what looked like tangled brown rope but smelled like something else. Just like Hilde, she put me on the long rope and made me run, both directions, until I was sweaty. Then she took the brown rope and stood next to me, rubbing my neck.

I watched the tangle as she brought it to my face. I felt something rubbing my gums. Could she be playing with my mouth? No one ever did that. They didn't like it when I played back. I opened up to taste whatever was being fed to me and felt a bendy stick on my tongue. Rusty and Wendy's talk about bits came back to me, and I tried to remember what they said. Or at least what Wendy said. I liked my half-brother but he might not always tell the truth.

The bendy stick was hard, but felt like two pieces. It tasted a little like the metal poles on my stall, only a little sweeter. The tangle was placed around my head. I figured out why soon. It was attached to the bit, which now stayed in my mouth. I learned this was called the bridle. There were two long pieces of brown rope called reins attached to the bit as well.

I chewed and licked as much as I could, while Auntie Niki patted my neck. She didn't call me a good boy as much as Hilde, but I could tell from her patting that I was doing okay. We stayed like this a little while, until I got used to it.

That's when she got into the saddle. It was just like Hilde with the ropes on my halter, only this time there were ropes coming from my mouth.

Auntie Niki asked me to walk, so I took some steps. It felt weird to have my mouth pulled right and left, and it took me a while to figure out what she was asking. I thought about what Wendy said about riders and their balance. Auntie Niki felt like she was sitting right over my backbone, but I would feel her a little heavier to the right when she pulled the right rein and a little heavier left when she pulled the left rein. This must be what Wendy was talking about.

We worked for a little while in the wood pen, Auntie Niki making me turn left and right, and stop, and walk. Just when I was getting tired, she stopped me, patted me again, then got off the saddle.

"Good Snoop," she said, and led me back to be put away.

That evening, I didn't talk about the bit too much. After everything I had already learned, it didn't seem like such a big deal. I mentioned it to Wendy.

"It was just like you said," I told her.

"You should see the one they use on Bubba," Rusty said, his mouth full of hay. "It's huge."

"That may be." Wendy stopped eating and walked to her water. "But watch him in the arena. His reins are very loose and his riders barely tug on the bit, if at all."

I considered what she said. "Then why make him wear the big bit if they don't use it?"

Wendy sighed. "I have no idea. Humans baffle me." She turned back to her feed, signaling an end to our talk.

I went back to my dinner, thinking about bits, and wondering if they'd make me wear anything big. I wasn't afraid, though. They had never done anything to hurt me.

CHAPTER THIRTEEN

Now Hilde only got me out on the days I wasn't ridden. Auntie Niki had taken over my training. The ranch had two arenas and I could see horses being ridden in both of them, but we were still in the wood pen. Every day looked the same. Walk, turn left and right, trot, turn right and left, stop, go, stop again, back up. I wondered if I would ever be ridden anywhere else. I overheard MomToo ask that question one day.

"We'll take him out when I've got steering and brakes," Auntie Niki told her.

I admit I was a little offended. I thought I went right and left like she said, sooner or later, and as for brakes, I stopped every time, mostly. But just like Hilde, Auntie Niki knew best, so we kept going back to the wood pen for more lessons.

One day, Auntie Niki had bounced her legs on me, making me trot. I trotted around the wood pen, feeling the reins slapping on my neck as I stuck my nose out and pushed my body forward, two opposite feet at a time. At some point, I felt her legs bounce harder, so I trotted faster. Then her leg nearest the wall started to bounce and rub on me while she made kissing noises with her mouth.

When I was on the long rope, this was my signal to run, but I couldn't imagine she wanted me to gallop. She kept asking and asking and wouldn't give up, so finally I gave her a slow lope, leading the way with my front inside leg. It was weird to run with the extra weight of a saddle and a person and I would have liked to buck a little, but I didn't. I figured it would be too hard.

We loped around a few times, then she slowed me down to a trot, then a walk and we reversed directions. Once again, she asked for the trot, then used her outside leg to perk me up into a lope on the opposite side. This was my left side and it was a little harder to do, so I kept trotting, then loping, then trotting again. We spent a few minutes on each side, then Auntie Niki stopped me, got off, and patted me.

Loping was added to our lessons and we spent each training day in the wood pen, practicing. The days ran into one another, from warm weather, to cold. I decided we'd never leave the wood pen. I tried to find something interesting about each time, but it was hard to stay focused.

One morning, after we had our training, Auntie Niki led me to the upper arena instead of going back to the barn. We sometimes did this. She would stand and talk to the other humans there, then take me back to be unsaddled.

Imagine my surprise when she took me into the arena and got back in my saddle. We were in a real arena at last. I was very excited, but tried to be good. She asked me to walk, so I did. There were other horses being ridden around me, but they didn't want to talk. They were busy working. I put my nose forward and tried to look like I was working, too.

It's funny how a different place makes your brain feel all soft and mushy. Auntie Niki and I had practiced turning and stopping in the wood pen forever, but somehow when she asked me to trot and tried to turn me in the bigger arena, I forgot how. Instead, I stuck my head up in the air and tried to wriggle my mouth away from her pulling. If she tried to pull my face down and turn me, I stopped. Each time I did that, she would push me forward into the trot and we'd try it again.

It took a few more days of being ridden in the arena before I could pay attention to her and be a good horse. After my mind calmed down, I remembered my lessons and it was easier. I learned that staying against the fence was called being *on the rail*. Each day, I would be walked and trotted on the rail, then in circles in the center of the arena. I liked it a lot. It was really easy.

Until the day we loped. I had gotten pretty good at it in the wood pen. She tapped me forward with one leg and I understood. I'd push off with my outside hind hoof and reach out with the inside front one. The arena was so much bigger than the wood pen, and I could go straight forever before I had to turn.

Auntie Niki asked me to lope down the rail on my left lead. I started really well. Then I started thinking about what I was doing. I felt happy to be loping such a long way in the arena. It was like I was free.

Loping... I'm loping! Here I go—loping!

I'm afraid I lost track of everything then, even my rider. I was running down the edge of the arena. Auntie Niki was pulling on the reins, but I stuck my head in the air and ignored her. It was fun until she finally got control of me again and made me slow down.

Miss Tina was walking past when it happened.

"Damned horse ran off with me," Auntie Niki said as she made me walk.

"Yeah, but his legs were moving so slow," Miss Tina told her. "And his knees were nice and flat."

It turned out that having Miss Tina watch me gave her ideas, even if I was out of control.

Look at me in the big arena.

CHAPTER FOURTEEN

Even before I was ridden in the arena, I used to get my hooves trimmed sometimes. A man named Monte would come and put me in the cross-ties, then pick up each hoof and clip a little off the bottom. He'd smooth my hooves down with a metal stick and lead me back to my stall.

At first, I didn't understand why he wanted to do this. I had been taught from my early days to let people pick up each hoof and hold it, but no one wanted to do anything more than clean the dirt out. Still, he seemed like an interesting human and it didn't hurt, so I was happy to let him do it. The first time, I reached over to grab his shirt with my teeth, but he slapped me on my bottom so hard I decided not to try that again. Ever.

When Auntie Niki and Miss Tina weren't in the arena riding, they sometimes stood around our stalls with groups of small humans and talked about us. I learned from listening that our hooves were like their fingernails, only thicker, and had to be trimmed so we could walk without hurting.

One day, after Auntie Niki had finished riding me in the big arena, Monte came and led me from my stall. His truck was next to the cross-ties as usual. It had a lot of interesting silver things in it, and part of it looked like it was on fire all the time. I always wanted to know what the silver things tasted like, but I didn't like the heat from the fire.

Monte trimmed my hooves and smoothed them, so I expected to go back to my stall. Suddenly, I felt something hard against my hoof. I watched Monte take one of the silver things and put it in the fire. When he took it out, it was red.

He pounded the red-silver thing with a stick, then stuck it in a bucket of water until it was silver again. The water made hissing noises.

Then he walked back over to me and put the silver thing on my foot again. It didn't hurt, but I could smell burning hair. I stuck my nose out and curled my lip to smell it more. I don't know why. It smelled awful.

He did this over and over, sticking the silver thing in the fire, then pounding it and putting it in the bucket, before holding it against my foot. I thought he was going to do this forever.

Finally, he stopped. I heard more pounding noises, and felt my foot get heavier. When he put my foot down, I saw the silver thing attached to the bottom of my hoof.

I was getting shoes.

There was a lot more heating and pounding for each shoe, then he used the rough stick to smooth everything down. At last, I was led out of the cross-ties by Monte's helper. He made me walk back and forth, then trot back and forth, then he took me back to my stall. My feet felt heavy, like they pulled on my legs with each step.

"Shoes," Rusty said. "Now you're a working horse for sure."

"They're heavy," I told him. "My legs are tired already."

"Yeah, they're heavy at first, but you get used to them." Rusty twirled around in his stall. "Soon you'll be back to running and jumping around."

"I don't think I ran and jumped around much before."

"Whatever. The thing is, now the humans will have to protect you from your own feet."

I didn't understand this. "How do they protect me? From what?"

"Oh I don't know. They put a bunch of stuff on your legs and hooves."

"What kind of stuff?" I asked.

"I don't know," he said. "Just stuff. I like to try to rip it off with my teeth."

"Don't pay any attention to him." Wendy turned to me. "Now that you have shoes, you can hurt yourself in a couple of ways. You can accidentally kick your own leg with the opposite foot, or some horses run so big, they can step on their front shoes with their back feet and rip the shoes off. To protect us, humans put things on our legs.

"They put bell boots on our front hooves so we don't pull off our shoes. Then they either put splint boots or polo wraps on our lower legs to keep us from hurting ourselves if we accidentally clip our leg with the other foot."

It was nice of Wendy to explain things to me. The next day, when Auntie Niki put things on my front feet before taking me to the wood pen, I knew I was wearing bell boots. And Rusty was right, too. It was fun to try to rip them off with my teeth.

CHAPTER FIFTEEN

Soon I learned to settle down in the big arenas and Auntie Niki didn't ride me in the wood pen anymore. Instead, I was ridden in both the upper and lower arenas. While she rode me, Miss Tina watched.

"Let's see how he likes the poles," she said one day and got into my saddle.

I could tell there was someone else on my back. Miss Tina has balance, too, but she rode different from Auntie Niki. There wasn't the same weight and she held the reins differently. I suppose if I weren't a horse, I could think of the right words to explain it. But she was not the same.

She asked me to walk toward a pole that was lying on the ground. I didn't know what she wanted me to do with it at first and thought she might let me pick it up in my teeth. I reached out my neck and put my nose to the ground, waiting to feel that painted wood in my mouth. Instead, she pushed her legs on me and made me keep walking. I had to lift my hooves to get over the pole.

It was kind of fun, so she tried another pole, and another. Each time, I walked over them very carefully, without kicking them. I started looking for the next pole, then the next one. If I couldn't eat them or throw them, walking over them seemed like fun.

Before long, I was trotting over poles, too, and eventually even loping over them. This became a great game, figuring out which direction Miss Tina was going to tell me to go and getting over the poles without touching them. In time, I learned to walk over a bridge, to back around cones and between poles, and to stand and let her open a gate, walk through, and close it.

In the meantime, MomToo watched me from the side of the arena. She didn't ride me very much. When Auntie Niki was training me, she would get on after my lesson and walk me around a little, but that was all.

The first time she rode me, I was tired after Auntie Niki's ride. I felt MomToo's soft legs tap-tap-tapping my sides so I walked forward. She stopped tapping, so I stopped moving. Then she tapped again, so I walked again. When she stopped, I stopped. We went around the arena this way for a few minutes. I thought maybe I didn't understand her, but when we ended and she got off the saddle, I could feel how happy she was.

MomToo felt different from everyone else. Sometimes it seemed like she wanted me to go to the left, but when I tried, she corrected me. That's when I started to understand what Wendy was telling me about a rider's balance.

Poor Wendy. MomToo wasn't off-balance much, and when she was, she fixed herself. But according to Wendy, her riders were always too far on one side or the other and she always had to figure out what they wanted.

That's too much like work. I like having fun better.

By the time I was three years old, Miss Tina was the only one riding me. She and MomToo talked about horse shows and something called a foo-chertee. I didn't know what they meant. I asked Wendy and Rusty about it. Rusty didn't know, but Wendy had a little idea.

"A horse show is a big place where there are a lot of horses and humans and it's very noisy and busy. You are in a different stall, where nothing tastes like home and there are strange neighbors to bother you. Your rider takes you to a special arena where humans are watching you and they make you do things. It's scary and awful and I never liked it."

"How do you get there?" I asked.

"In the big box that moves."

I had never heard of that before. "A moving box?"

"It has food inside and usually it's you and a few other horses. The floors go up and down and you can see the trees going sideways from the window. When the stall stops moving, you're in a new place."

"Wow, that sounds like fun."

"Not really. You get tired of standing in one place and the floor can make your legs feel sore. But at least you get to eat."

Wendy didn't want to talk about it anymore, but at least I knew what a horse show was. That is, until I talked to Bubba.

He was an older horse, a sorrel with a white blaze, and didn't like to talk much when we stood together getting brushed and saddled. One day, I heard his rider talk about going to a show, so I asked him about it.

"Are they as awful and frightening as Wendy says?"

"Absolutely not. Horse shows are the best things. I love to go to them. You get a bath and a haircut, and humans come and tell you how handsome you are. Then you go out to the arena and do your job and humans come and tell you how spectacular you did. They give you ribbons and prizes."

Wendy didn't tell me about the ribbons and prizes. I wondered if I could eat them or throw them.

"Well, what's a foo-chertee?"

"It's *futurity*," he corrected me. "It's a special class for young horses, usually three-year-olds, who are good, but still learning. I was in futurity classes when I was your age. I was spectacular." He puffed up his chest a little when he said this.

I wasn't sure what *spectacular* meant, but Bubba was very proud of it, so it must be a good thing.

Now I knew what Miss Tina and MomToo were talking about. I was going to a horse show to be in a futurity class. After listening to Bubba, this sounded exciting. And I wanted to see that big moving box.

One morning after my lesson, I went to live in a stall in the barn. This one wasn't made of metal poles to let me look out everywhere. The walls were all made of wood, and the door was the only place I could see out of. It was metal and I could hang my head over it.

When I looked around, there were lots of horses in this barn. Most of them had their heads over their stall doors. They looked a lot different from Johnny and Tucker, and especially Uncle Snowy. They were taller and their coats were shiny. Bubba was here in this barn, too.

MomToo visited me later that evening. "You're a show horse now, Snoopy. You get a fancy indoor stall."

She walked inside with a big red cloth. At first, she kind of held it up to me, so I reached out and grabbed it and she pulled it away.

"Not food," she said. "This is a blanket."

Then she put it on my back. It felt weird and I still wanted to know what it was, so when she reached under my belly to get a strap, I grabbed the blanket with my teeth and pulled it off.

"Quit." She sounded mad and yanked the blanket back.

This was a fun game, so I did it a couple more times, until MomToo got tired of it. She put my halter on and led me out of my stall, then put the blanket on me again. When I turned to grab it, she tugged my lead rope and made me face forward.

The game was over. I stood still and let her fasten the blanket under my belly and through my back legs. She put me back in my stall and took my halter off.

I didn't think much about it until the next morning. When the ranch man came to clean my stall, he took my blanket off. Brrr, I was cold. I decided it was a good thing to have a blanket on at night.

MomToo's first ride.

CHAPTER SIXTEEN

I didn't have to wait long to find out about the big moving box. One morning, very early, Auntie Niki came and got me out. I hadn't even had my breakfast yet. She led me to a big metal box that was making thump-a-thump noises. I stood still and let her take my blanket off, then she walked to the open end of the box.

I followed and looked in.

It was dark inside, but I could smell a bunch of things. There was a shavings smell and the smell of other horses. Most importantly, there was hay. Auntie Niki walked up a slanted floor and tugged on my lead rope. I was happy to go eat hay, even if it was kind of dark in there.

Once inside, she tied me to the box and closed a gate. I was already eating when I heard the thump-a-thump noise again. A horse was moving around next to me.

"Who are you?" I asked.

"Bubba. Is that Snoopy?"

"Yes. Is this the big moving box? Are we going to a horse show? Will we be in a futurity?" It was hard to talk and eat at the same time, but I had so many questions.

"This is a horse trailer, but if you want to call it a big moving box, that's okay with me. Yes, we're going to a horse show. I don't know what you'll do there, but I will not be in a futurity. They're for three-year olds. I'm thirteen."

I heard hooves on the other side. It was Rusty. We stood there, eating, forever, before a noise startled me. It sounded like Miss Tina's truck. Sometimes she drove it past my stall to unload hay. It always made a grumbling noise and smelled bad.

Suddenly, the floor started to go up and down under my feet, and I saw our barn go sideways. Then I didn't see our barn anymore. I saw trees going sideways. The big box was moving.

We moved forever. At first, it was fun, but then I ran out of food, so I started chewing on my lead rope and shifting my weight back and forth.

Bubba told me to stop it. "Just close your eyes and get some sleep."

"I'm not sleepy."

"Snoopy." He said my name like he was trying not to be mad and kick at me. "This is your first horse show. I barely remember my first show, but I've seen a lot of young horses. Being in a different place will make you either excited or frightened. Being in a different stall, where you have new neighbors and nothing smells or tastes the same will make it hard for you to rest. Sleep as much as you can now, or you will regret it."

I didn't know what regret meant, but it sounded like something I wouldn't like, so I closed my eyes. I didn't sleep, but I did close my eyes.

When we stopped, it was getting dark outside. I could feel Rusty stomping his feet next to me and calling out.

"Hey, where are we? Who's out there? Why are we still in this box?"

He made Bubba mad. "Tell him to shut up. We'll get into our stalls when they're ready."

I passed the information to my half-brother. "Bubba says to shut up. We'll set on our tails when they're pretty."

"That's not what I said."

"Sorry," I told him. "Rusty got me a little confused with his yelling. He's not listening to me anyway."

After forever, I heard the back door of the box open. Rusty stopped yelling. Horse hooves were stomping on the slanted floor. Then I heard metal clanging, then more horse hooves. At last, the clanging sound was next to me and I saw light. Auntie Niki untied my rope.

"I see you chewed on this," she said, and asked me to back up.

I'm used to walking backward. Hilde taught me when I was little. The floor felt funny. It creaked and moved a little when I stepped. Then I stepped out and didn't feel floor at all. I stopped, but Auntie Niki kept clucking at me and tugging back on my rope. It was weird, but I finally felt the floor, only it was lower. Then I remembered walking up a slanted piece to get into the moving box and understood.

She was asking me to go backward on the slanted floor. It was hard, but I kept moving my feet backward.

At last I was out of the box and on the ground. Auntie Niki led me to a stall. It had shavings and a light on, just like home. Instead of a bowl that gave me a drink when I put my nose inside, there were two buckets filled with water. I drank a little, but it didn't taste like the water at home. More important was the big hunk of hay in the corner, all for me.

I could hear Miss Tina and Auntie Niki clanging and banging stuff. Rusty was yelling again, but I didn't care. I had food. I stuck my head out of the stall a couple of times to see where we were. The big moving box was in my way. All I could see was the corner of an arena to my left and a bunch of big wheeled things to my right.

"Bubba?" I tried not to scream, but it was hard to be heard over Rusty.

"What?"

"Now what happens?"

"Now we eat and go to sleep. In the morning, we'll be longed and ridden."

That sounded good. I was still eating my dinner when Auntie Niki came in and put my blanket on. I guessed it would be time to sleep soon. As she left, she closed the top and bottom doors of my stall. There was a light on, so I wasn't scared. The shavings smelled different than the ones in my stall at home, but they still looked comfy to me. I finished my dinner and eased myself down into the shavings. Closing my eyes, I tried to ignore Rusty, who was still running circles in his stall and yelling about everything.

After forever he got tired, I guess, and stopped, which was good. I wanted to take Bubba's advice, but a guy can't sleep with so much noise around him.

CHAPTER SEVENTEEN

In the morning, I ate my breakfast, then hung my head out of the stall. The big moving box was gone, so I got to see lots of open space. There were new horses to look at and humans walking by. They were all so interesting, I spent most of the morning looking at everything that happened outside my door.

Just when I was starting to wonder about what Bubba said, Miss Tina came and pulled my blanket off, then put my halter on. She tied me in my stall. I thought this was silly and kept moving around. Being tied in my stall meant I couldn't look outside. Soon, she brought the saddle and pad. I stood still for her to put them on, then I got excited and started swinging my butt around and nodding my head.

She came back with the long rope and the whip. I knew what happened next. We'd go to a wood pen and I could run. We walked for a long, long way that felt like forever and I kept chewing on the chain and the rope and she kept pulling it out of my mouth. We finally got to a big arena and she led me inside.

I was confused. At home, I run on the long rope in a wood pen, not the arenas. But she sent me from her and waved the whip, so I ran. I jumped and bucked and nearly fell down on my knees, it felt so good to run. Even though it wasn't very hot outside, I got pretty sweaty running. I ran forever, until Miss Tina stopped me and put my bridle on. Then she got on and rode me around the arena.

Afterward, we went back to our stalls and she took off the saddle. We walked to a big, big wash rack, where she hosed me off. This wash rack let me move around on my lead rope, which was fun. I got to swing my body from side to side and play with the water.

Miss Tina didn't like that so much and kept pushing me over and telling me to stop. Humans can be strict.

Back in my stall, I watched Bubba's owner get him out and put his saddle on. He wore two pads with spots on them and a shiny saddle. This made me curious.

"Bubba, why are you wearing so many pads?"

"The top pad is called a Navajo. It matches my rider's clothes."

"Why are there spots on the back of it?"

"Spots?" He looked back at his pads. "Those aren't spots. Those are my numbers. That's how the judges recognize and score me."

"Judges?"

"Oh, Snoopy, what you don't know." His owner came and put a big bit in his mouth, with a shiny bridle. "I'll try to explain when I return," he said as she led him away.

I waited forever for him to come back. Auntie Niki fed me, so that took some time. I watched Rusty leave with her, saddled and on the long rope, then come back sweaty but still acting silly. The big dark horse, Jet, was with us, too. He liked being chased by a wheeled thing. Bubba called it a cart. I was glad I didn't have to be chased by it, no matter what it was called. Jet didn't talk much.

"He's conceited," Bubba had said.

"What's that mean?" I asked.

"It means he thinks he's too good to talk to us."

"I'm not conceited." Jet didn't even put his head out of the stall, so we could barely hear him. "I just don't like other horses, unless they're mares."

I guess I should have felt bad about him not liking me, but it was okay. I like everyone. It doesn't matter if they like me or not.

Finally, after forever, Bubba came back. He got his saddle off, then went away and returned wet. Even his tail was all wet and I noticed little bugs in his mane.

"They're not bugs, they're rubber bands," he explained. "When you go into the show arena, you must be very clean, from your ears to your tail. Your nose and ears and feet are all clipped so you look sleek. Then your mane is banded, which means they put rubber bands around little sections, all the way down your neck. When you are all dressed and ready, you go into the arena and perform with your rider for the judges."

"What's 'perform' mean?"

"If you are in an arena with cones, you perform a pattern. If you are in an arena with nothing in it, you go around the rail and perform pleasure. If you are in an arena with poles, you perform trail."

"I like the poles." I watched his owner brush his tail. "What are judges?"

"They're humans who watch you and say that you are a winner."

"Are you always a winner?"

"No." Bubba snorted. "But that is not my fault. Sometimes the judges do not understand I'm the best."

"When will I go into the arena and perform for judges?"

He looked me up and down. "Since you have not had a bath or bands put in your mane, I think you will not show here."

"Why wouldn't I?"

"Probably because it is your first show. They want to see if you will be a good and quiet show horse, or a crazy one." He glanced toward Rusty's stall as he said this.

I watched him go back into his stall. Auntie Niki was giving everyone more hay, so we all started eating. I couldn't believe they weren't going to dress me up and take me into the big arena. I was at a horse show. Of course, I was going to show.

Bubba was right. We were there forever, seven whole nights, and all I did was go to the arena with a bunch of horses, run around on the rope, then get ridden. When the big moving box came to take us home, I was sad.

I hoped there would be more shows. After talking with Bubba, I knew I had a lot more to learn.

CHAPTER EIGHTEEN

When we got back home, we went back to normal, sort of. Every day, I ran around the wood pen, then Miss Tina rode me over the poles. Only now, she acted more serious. She had never liked it when I tried to play, like grabbing at the lead rope or chewing the reins. But now I got into major trouble when I didn't mind my manners.

Honest, I try to be a good horse. I just forget.

Good thing the poles were still fun. I loved trying to figure out where we would go and how to take the right number of steps and not hit anything with my feet. Walk into the box and turn left, then walk out and jog right, left, right, pick up left lead over the fan. Sometimes she picked up on the reins and made me go slower. And sometimes we'd fight about opening the gate.

I was supposed to stand still at the gate while she picked up the rope, then back up, walk through the posts, back up again, and stand still to let her hang up the rope. I knew what to do and I wanted to go ahead and do it. She seemed to think I should wait for her to tell me. I thought she should trust me. I had this.

One afternoon, Auntie Niki brought me into the barn and took out the clippers. I've been clipped lots of times. The clippers make a buzzy noise and rub on my nose and I like to lick them. Auntie Niki smacks me. I lick, she smacks, I lick again. It's a good game. When she's finished, my long muzzle hairs are gone.

This time, she rubbed it all over my nose and mouth as usual, tapping me and telling me to quit licking. Then she moved my halter and ran the clippers on my bridle path, which is between my ears.

Suddenly, she grabbed one of my ears. I heard and felt the buzzing of the clippers and tried to move my head out of the way, but she had my ear and kept rubbing. After forever, she patted my neck and told me I was a good boy. That wasn't so bad, until she moved to the other side and grabbed the other ear. I tried to escape again, but she kept clipping forever until she stopped and patted me again.

She put away the clippers, and I thought I could go back to my stall. Then she pulled out big clippers and started rubbing my legs, down near my hooves. It was a little ticklish, but not as bad as on my ears, so I stood still and let her clip my legs. When she was done, my legs felt like there was no hair on them. It was okay. I finally went back to my stall, wondering why she clipped so much of me.

The next morning, Miss Tina led me out of my stall, to the big moving box. Bubba was already there. Rusty wasn't around, or Jet, but a sorrel named BuddyTwo was in the box. He lived in a different barn, so I didn't know him very well.

"Hi, my name's Snoopy," I told him.

"Shut up and stay away from my food," he replied.

I thought maybe he was grumpy because he didn't get to eat all his breakfast. There was a full bag of hay in front of me, as well as a window to watch the trees go sideways, so I was happy.

The floor went up and down and the trees went sideways for a long time. When we stopped, we were in front of different stalls. It wasn't like the other place at all. This place had a lot of trees. The stalls faced the other way, but they were wood, with doors that opened on the top and the bottom. Auntie Niki took me out right away and longed me. It felt so good. I ran and ran and ran, until I was sweaty.

I thought we were done, but Miss Tina saddled me and rode me around for a while. When I was really, really tired, she took me to the wash rack and gave me a full bath. I've never been scrubbed so hard, but it felt like the best back scratch ever.

We went back to my stall, and I was happy, until she tied me up. I hate being tied up, and kept moving around and chewing the lead rope.

I did that forever, until Auntie Niki came back and got me out. She tied me outside my stall door, and then she did a weird thing. She stood on a box and put rubber bands in my mane. I wanted to help her, or at least taste her shirt, or stand on the box, but Auntie Niki wouldn't let me. Every time I tried to have fun, she tugged on my halter or slapped my neck. I didn't like the tugging and slapping, so I tried to stand still, except that I kept forgetting and moving around and getting spanked again.

When it was all done, Auntie Niki put a special, tight blanket on my head and neck. It hooked around my chest, and there were holes for my eyes, ears, and muzzle. Then she put me in my stall for the evening. There was a big pile of hay waiting for me, so I ate it. Afterward, I stuck my head out of my stall and looked over at Bubba, who had a blanket on his face just like me.

"You look like you're ready for the show," he said.

"Why are we wearing blankets on our faces?"

"Blankets?" He snorted at me. "These things are called sleazies. They keep the bands straight in our manes and help us stay clean."

"Oh." I thought about why Auntie Niki would do this. "Am I going to perform for the judges?"

"Yes. I heard them talk about it."

That made me very excited. "Is this the futurity? What am I going to perform?"

"How should I know? What does your rider do with you at home?"

"Miss Tina rides me over poles."

"Then you will do trail, like me."

I thought about all the times Bubba and I were in the arena at home, going over poles. "Will we be judged together?"

"No. I am in the class for experienced horses. You will be in the class for beginning horses."

"But I'm not a beginning horse. I've gone over poles before."

I heard him snort again. "Yes, but this is your first time being judged. You haven't been in a horse show before."

BuddyTwo interrupted us. "Can you two shut up? I'm trying to sleep here."

It was kind of sad to see him so grumpy, especially when I was so excited to be here. I was hoping he'd feel better when his owner got here to cheer him up.

Bubba moved back inside his stall, but I kept looking outside. There were new humans and horses all around us. Everything looked and smelled and tasted like it had never looked and smelled and tasted before. Bubba had said we were in a different city. I don't know what a city is, so it didn't matter to me. All that mattered was, I was going to perform for judges.

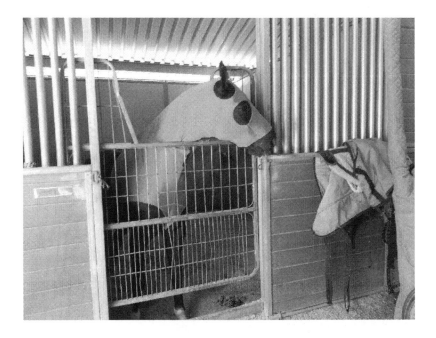

Me and my sleazie.

CHAPTER NINETEEN

The next day, Miss Tina got me out of my stall and took off my blanket and my sleazie. She brushed my coat until it was shiny, then she stood behind me with a bunch of long black hair in her hand. It looked like a horse's tail, if it had been on a horse.

"You got a pitiful tail, horse," she said, as she fastened the tail in her hand to my own.

It's true, my tail is not as thick and pretty as other horses' tails. Auntie Niki says I got it from Mom, and that I'm *follicularly challenged* whatever that means. I can still brush the flies off, so it's useful to me.

Now I had more hair, although the fastener kind of pulled at my tail bone and made everything feel heavier. It wasn't very good for swishing, either. I tried to remove a fly from my hip, and my real tail whooshed upward, while the fake one hung down like it was dead.

Miss Tina disappeared and came back with two pads and a sparkly saddle, which she put on my back. I looked around. It was just like what I saw on Bubba at the last show. I even had the spots he called numbers on my pads.

While Miss Tina was getting me ready, MomToo came. She was happy to see me, and petted me, then slapped me when I tried to rub her with my lips. Miss Tina left MomToo to put on my bridle and lead me away.

We walked over to the arena with the poles. I was excited, but I knew I needed to be a good horse. Still, I couldn't help putting the reins in my mouth. They are kind of soft and chewy and taste good.

MomToo smacked me in the chest, so I walked forward to touch her with my nose and apologize, but she yanked on the reins and made me back up. I keep forgetting no one wants me to touch them with my nose, mostly because if I like what I smell, I want to taste.

After forever, Miss Tina got in the saddle and made me walk and jog around. Then Auntie Niki came over and sprayed me with that funny smelling stuff to keep the flies away, and we walked toward the poles. We stood at the entrance and I watched a horse, all by himself, having fun with his rider on the poles, loping, jogging, walking. I wondered why we weren't going in with him, but Miss Tina made me stand still.

When that horse left, she asked me to walk in. Sometimes at home, we were the only ones in the arena, but this felt different. Humans were watching us, and Miss Tina didn't feel as relaxed as usual.

I could feel a little more excitement in her legs, like when the air feels all buzzy and MomToo talks about static electricity. At home, as we'd start toward a pole, she'd give me a little tug on the reins. Not here. She was giving me a lot of rein and pushing me with her legs over each pole.

We started over the first pole, walking, then picked up the jog and went left-right-left through cones, before loping the wheel. At home, sometimes I do things over and over, especially if I keep hitting the pole with my feet. Not here. We kept going from one set of poles to the next, right lead to jog to left lead to walk, until we got to the gate.

I tried to listen to her as she picked up the rope, but I knew what to do, so I kind of took over. She didn't stop me, and I didn't hit anything. Still, she was kind of mad about that. I could feel it through the saddle.

She walked me back to the entrance and we left the arena. I felt her patting my neck.

"He was good, for his first time," I heard her say.

She got off and handed my reins to MomToo. "He was a little ticky over that pole, and didn't want to listen at the gate, but other than that, I was happy. I'll take him in Junior Horse after this and see how he does."

MomToo held me for a while and we played our favorite games of *who's got the reins*, and *how close is too close*. At least they're *my* favorite games. After forever, Miss Tina came back and got in the saddle again.

Like before, we waited until there were no horses in the arena and then walked in. I could tell after the first pole that we were going to go the same direction we did last time, so I decided to look around and see what was on the outside of the arena. There were humans standing and watching. Some had horses with them, others had dogs, and lots were eating. I wanted to watch them, instead of watching where I was going. After all, I knew the path.

Suddenly, I felt my hoof rub against a pole and a sharp tug at my mouth. Miss Tina thought I should focus on the course. I thought she was being silly. I had already done it once. But I turned around and paid attention. I even slowed down and let Miss Tina work the gate without my help.

We finished, and I noticed a group of humans in chairs, sitting at the edge of the arena. Two of the humans wore big hats like Miss Tina, and they nodded at me as I walked past.

I couldn't wait to get back to the barn to ask Bubba about all this.

CHAPTER TWENTY

After forever, MomToo walked me back to my stall and took the saddle and pads off, and even the dead tail. Then she took out a little shiny thing and started to pull on my mane. I couldn't quite see what she was doing, and I kept moving around, trying to see and trying to get to my food and water. She kept slapping me and telling me to hold still.

It took a long time for whatever she was doing, and she had to reach real close to me. Once I stepped on her foot and that made her mad. She said some bad words, so I stopped moving for a second or two, until I forgot. At last, I felt her run her hand up and down my mane.

"There, I got all the bands," she said. "You're all done."

I didn't get another bath or my sleazie put on or anything. She unbuckled the halter and let me loose in my stall. The first thing I did was eat some of my hay. Then I stuck my head out and looked for Bubba.

He wasn't in his stall, so I called to BuddyTwo. He was home, and as cranky as usual.

"What?"

"I was in my first show today. It was fun."

"Good for you, kid."

"Why are you so unhappy? Horse shows are fun. You get to see new things and meet new horses."

He stuck his head out of the stall to my right. "This is your first show, but I know who you are. You've had one owner. A couple of trainers, all on the place you were born. I was at the same ranch, too, until I was three. Thought I'd stay there my whole life. Instead, I've been through dozens of hands, from big humans to little humans."

I already knew horses didn't always live in one place. I remembered what Uncle Snowy had told me about how nice our home was. "Were they mean humans?"

"No, none of them was ever mean. They just didn't love me. The little humans did, but it seems I could never stay with them. They grew bigger and then I'd hear the trainer say those words: *You've outgrown him and we need to find you a better horse.* At one time, I was the better horse. The little girl who rides me now loves me. But I know what's coming."

He looked over at me. "You have a big human, but I know she loves you."

"MomToo? Of course she loves me."

"I mean, she'll never sell you, never give you to anyone else."

I had never considered this. "Did she tell you that?"

"No, but I know. She bought your mom to show, but when your mom hated it, she bred her and got you. Most owners sell the baby and breed the mare again, but not your owner. She kept you and your mom, but she didn't make your mom have any more foals. When humans are like that, their horses are in their forever home."

We both ate for a while. Finally, he told me, "I know I sound cranky, but I'm twenty years old now. I'm done. I want to retire and stop all this nonsense."

I heard a call from the arena and saw Bubba walking back. It was nice to find out that BuddyTwo wasn't always so grumpy, but I was excited to tell Bubba about what I'd done earlier.

"That's really good," he said after I told him about the first time in the arena. When I told him about the second, he shook his head. "That won't do at all. When you are in the arena, you must listen to your rider. Otherwise they will not say your name and a number, and your rider will not be happy."

"What kind of name and number do they say?"

"Well, did you hear your name?"

I considered this. "They did say my big name, My Flashy Investment."

"Really? What did they say after?"

"One time they said my name and the word third and one time they said my name and the word sixth. What does that mean?"

"Well." He kind of coughed this, as his saddle was being removed. "When you are a first horse, your humans get very excited. When you are a second horse, they are not as excited, but they are very happy. They are just happy when you are a third or fourth horse. So you made your humans just happy."

That sounded good to me. I liked making everyone happy.

CHAPTER TWENTY-ONE

Much later, I found out that there were names to the places we went. I didn't really care, but MomToo and Miss Tina talked about it a lot, so I finally started listening. The first show I went to was called the Sun Circuit in Scottsdale, Arizona. The first show I showed in was in Bakersfield, California.

After Bakersfield, I was in the big moving box all the time, going to places named Del Mar and Watsonville and Paso Robles. Sometimes Bubba went with me, but sometimes I went alone. A few times, MomToo wasn't even there, so it was just me and Miss Tina. At home, I learned from Bubba that this was the futurity circuit.

I didn't know what a circuit was, but I guessed that meant a big bunch of horse shows.

At home, I went over more poles, every day. Miss Tina made me work a little harder each time, turning a little quicker and stopping a little sooner. We trotted over poles and loped over poles and walked and backed up and went through the gate forever, until we stopped.

Sometimes I got a little confused. We would trot over poles a bunch of times, until I figured out how many steps I needed to take to keep from hitting them with my hooves. I thought I was supposed to do everything by myself. But when we stopped at the gate and I tried to back and walk through without waiting to be told, Miss Tina would tug on my face and tell me no.

Wasn't I supposed to be helpful?

I also wasn't supposed to eat anything in the arena, and every time I reached for a flower or a bush, I got spanked. The flowers didn't taste good anyway, but they were fun to throw.

One day, Miss Tina had been making me turn around inside poles that were in the shape of a box, kind of like my stall except they were just big enough for me to stand in. I had to move my front feet, then my back feet, then my front again, all underneath me, in order to turn around. Finally, we walked over one of the poles and out of the box, and she turned me around to face where we had been.

I heard her say something about fixing a pole, then I felt her get out of the saddle and tie the rein so I couldn't grab it. She did this sometimes. I would usually stand still while she walked over to a pole and moved it.

That day, I wanted to try the box again. She had pointed me toward it, and I was trying to figure out whether I was supposed to do things on my own or not. So when she walked to the pole, I walked into the box, turned around, and walked out. That made her laugh. I don't know why, but it was okay.

I like making everyone happy.

Most days, we worked and then I got a shower, but I learned to tell when we were going in the big moving box. After Miss Tina rode me, Auntie Niki would get out the clippers. Sometimes she clipped my nose and my bridle path and put me back in my stall. But when she clipped my ears and my legs, I knew we were going to a show.

One morning she clipped my ears and legs, then MomToo came and gave me a big bath with lots of smelly suds. I was led to the cross-ties and stood in the sun. My skin was a little cold from the bath, so it felt good to be warmed. Bubba was in the cross-ties next to me.

"I think I'm going to another show," I told him. "Are you going, too?"

"Yes. It's the last show of the year, and a very important one for you."

This surprised me. "Why is it so important?"

"I heard them talking in the barn. This is the last futurity show, and you must be doing very well. They think you have a chance of winning."

Snoopy & Gayle Carline

I still didn't quite understand everything about shows. Maybe I ask stupid questions, but it's okay. I like to learn. "Bubba, what does winning mean?"

"It means the judges think, out of all the horses who did what you did, you did it best." He chuffed a little. "Did you hear your name and a number at these shows?"

"Sometimes." I had to admit, I wasn't always listening, especially if there was a plant to eat, or if my reins were close enough to grab. "I remember hearing I was a first horse, then I think a third horse. I forgot the rest."

"Well, then, this is the show where either you will win or you will not. It is your choice."

We were both quiet for a while. I would have to think about this. Winning was still strange to me. Did I care if humans thought I went over poles better than the other horses? Maybe not. Mostly, I liked to go over the poles because it was fun. After I left the arena, I liked to look for something to taste or grab. Hearing my name and a number wasn't interesting.

I did want to make humans happy, though, especially MomToo, and Miss Tina and Auntie Niki. If they wanted me to win, I guess I would try to win for them.

CHAPTER TWENTY-TWO

Early in the morning, I walked into the big moving box again. This time, I was the first horse. Bubba walked in behind me. I had been taken out of my stall before I finished my hay, so I was too busy grabbing mouthfuls from the bag in front of me to say much to my friend. I guess he was hungry, too, because he didn't say much more than a quick hello.

The floor had been moving up and down and the trees had been moving sideways for a long time before I was full.

"Is there a name to this place we are going?" I asked Bubba.

"Santa Barbara. It is the Fall Classic."

I took in all the words, even though I didn't understand them. I had something else on my mind. Something BuddyTwo had said to me back in Bakersfield.

"Bubba, have you had lots of owners?"

"A few. The lady who owns me now is number sixth."

"Did you… do you…" I was having trouble figuring out how to ask what I wanted to know. "BuddyTwo told me that I was loved, and that he knows I will always belong to my MomToo. Are you… are you loved?"

Bubba was quiet forever. I thought he had started eating again. Then he spoke.

"When I was born, I was handled by humans, but I was one of many colts. They sold me to other humans who trained me to be ridden, then sold me again. Everyone had time to make me do things correctly, but no one had time to reward me for my effort. If I was lucky and I had been good, I would get a pat on the neck. If I was not good, I would get… disciplined."

He said the last word sadly.

"What's disciplined?"

"Tied in my stall for hours without food or water. Beaten with the whip. Ridden in circles with spurs digging into my sides and my head being held down to my chest. Things no horse should have to endure."

This sounded bad. I had been tied in my stall sometimes, but always where I could at least drink. And humans had chased me around the wood pen by waving the whip and making it crackle, but no one ever beat me with it.

"When I was bought by my current owner, Miz Cee, I expected more of the same. For a long time, I was very nervous. She wanted to pet me and kiss my nose and feed me treats. No one had ever done that, and I didn't know what I was supposed to do. The worst part was when she or Tina rode me.

"I was trained to stay on the rail. If I moved away, I was beaten. When Miz Cee started riding me in the middle of the arena, I got so nervous and afraid of the punishment I was going to get, that I bucked her off a couple of times. Then I waited for the beating I was used to getting for being bad.

"But she didn't. She never hurt me, even though I hurt her. She got back on and tried again. I can barely believe that now I can go in the middle of the arena, and even go over poles, and not worry. I've never been—disciplined—by Miz Cee or Tina. Some days, I still get nervous about things. It's hard to forget what used to happen when I did something wrong.

"But, yes, Snoopy. I am loved. At last, I am loved."

He was quiet again, so I looked into my bag for more hay. There was some at the bottom. I dug my face in, trying to reach it, when I heard him talking.

"And you, Snoopy, are a lucky horse. You live with your mother on the ranch where you were born, and from the first day, you were encouraged and rewarded for being good. But you've got to stop grabbing everything that comes into your space. It is the only time I see them spank you, not that they spank you hard. But you've got to stop."

"I try, Bubba," I said, chewing the last bit of alfalfa. "But everything is so interesting, and I want to know what it all is. I don't know any other way to get to know things."

"Then you are doubly lucky, because your owner loves you anyway."

After forever, I felt the floor stop moving and saw stalls outside. I tried to wait quietly, but when they took Bubba and I was the last horse, I started yelling, so they wouldn't forget and leave me in the moving box.

"Knock it off," said Auntie Niki, as she opened the wall and untied my lead rope.

As usual, I backed down the slanted floor, then walked to my stall. I saw I was next to Bubba, so I was happy. Our first day was spent like any other show day. We ate a little hay while Miss Tina and Auntie Niki took things from the moving box, like saddles and bridles and a cart full of brushes, and put them in an empty stall. When they were done, Miss Tina got into her truck and drove away with the moving box.

One by one, we all were taken out of our stalls, longed, ridden, and bathed. When I went out, I heard Bubba calling for me, so when he went out, I called for him. In the afternoon, MomToo came and took me out of my stall. She tried to hold me still while Auntie Niki banded me. I tried to grab her shirt and hat with my teeth. After a while, she held my lead rope up to my mouth, so I took that and chewed on it.

"This is probably not a good idea," she told Auntie Niki.

"I know," Auntie Niki said, "but if it keeps him still, I'm all for it."

At last, I had my sleazie and my blanket on, and more food was served. The sky got dark and Bubba's owner came around and closed our stall top doors. It was time to rest. Tomorrow I would show for the judges, and I had to try to win.

CHAPTER TWENTY-THREE

In the morning I got more food, which always makes it a good morning. MomToo came as I finished and got me out of my stall, brushed and saddled me. Miss Tina then took me to the arena and we worked on the trail course.

I had learned this was not for the judges. There were lots of horses on the course and everyone was going everywhere. It was a little hard to pay attention to Miss Tina because there were so many voices. The humans were giving instructions to other humans and to horses. Some of the horses were chatty, too, asking who everyone was and worrying about the course and their riders.

Bubba was out, with his owner. He was silent. I called to him, but he shushed me and said he had work to do. I shut up, too, and focused on Miss Tina's balance and legs. We went over all the poles, one group at a time. After forever, she was happy and MomToo took me back to the barn, unsaddled me, and tied me in my stall. I ate and drank, and waited.

The sun was higher when MomToo took me out and saddled me again. This time I had the shiny saddle and numbers. I knew what that meant. It was time to win.

At some shows, everything happened really fast. We'd go to the arena and Miss Tina would ride me over some poles, then we'd step up to the judges. They'd nod at me, and I would start.

Some shows were really slow. We'd stand in the arena forever. Sometimes Miss Tina would hold my reins and sometimes MomToo or Auntie Niki would do it. It was hard to stand still. I usually forgot that I wasn't supposed to chew on the reins or grab anyone's shirt or hat, or lick the dirt.

"Snoopy, you wear me out," MomToo would tell me.

This day was a slow show. We stood and stood. MomToo kept brushing my coat and wiping my eyes, and fussing with my tail. When she had smacked me with the reins about the forevereth time, Miss Tina came and got on me. We went around the back part of the arena and went over some poles, both fast and slow. At last, she steered me toward the judges.

The course was super easy. I had plenty of time to lope over the poles and look around at things. There wasn't much to see, although I did see MomToo and Auntie Niki watching us. We jogged the crooked poles, left, right, left, then stopped at the gate.

I knew what to do here. I suppose I should have been a good horse, but I was excited, and wanted to show off. Miss Tina picked up the rope. It's hard to wait for her. Sometimes she asks me to back up right away, and sometimes she makes me stop for a while. I decided that the judges needed to see us in action, so I started backing without waiting for her to ask.

In my excitement, I'm afraid I let my back feet swing wide, instead of placing them carefully. Miss Tina tried to make me angle away from the gate, but she was a little late. I felt half of the gate move.

This was bad.

I walked through the gate and backed up, again, without Miss Tina's instructions, trying to get it over with and prove I knew what I was doing. At least I didn't move anything else. We finished the course and the judges nodded.

"I don't know what got into him," Tina said as she got down from my saddle. "Suddenly, he thought he'd take over." She said a lot more that I didn't understand, about the number of points we had and there was only one other horse who could beat us.

Usually, someone takes me back to the barn and unsaddles me, but today we all stood and watched the other horses, then listened for the voice to say my name and number.

I heard lots of names and lots of numbers. When they got to "My Flashy Investment," they said I was seventh horse. I remembered what Bubba said. He didn't even mention the number seventh.

"Well, that ties us up, I think," Tina said. "It's all going to depend on tomorrow's course."

MomToo took me back to the barn. She wasn't as happy as if I was a first horse, but she didn't seem sad. I still got a nice bath, some hay, and even an apple.

"How did you do?" Bubba asked as he was being saddled.

I told him.

"Snoopy, Snoopy, Snoopy. You must let your rider decide what to do next. They are your leader."

"Why do we need a leader? Can't everyone figure out what to do and do it?"

He snorted. "Yes, they can, but the leader tells you when. Besides, your rider can see the edge of the gate, sometimes better than you. Let them help you keep your big feet out of the way. Don't you want to win?"

I shook my head. "I do. Tomorrow I will be better."

That night, I dreamed I knocked all the poles down and everyone was sad. I heard Miss Tina say that MomToo had outgrown me and needed a better horse. It woke me up. I was not going to be the *not better* horse. I was going to pick up my feet and listen to Miss Tina. I was going to win for MomToo. Somehow, I managed to go back to sleep.

CHAPTER TWENTY-FOUR

The next day, everything happened as usual. Food, longeing, riding, more food. The sun was in the same place when I was taken to the show arena. This time, Auntie Niki held me.

MomToo said, "I'm going up to the stands. Maybe I fussed with him too much yesterday."

I wasn't sure what she meant, but I watched her walk over to the place above us in the arena, where lots of humans were sitting and watching. There was a piece of my rein near the corner of my mouth, so I sucked it in and began chewing. Auntie Niki took it away from me. I scooted forward to lean my chin on her shoulder, so I could maybe scratch her with my teeth, but she backed me up.

We stood like this forever, me grabbing at stuff and her stopping me. Maybe Bubba was right, and I was lucky to have humans who would put up with me. Or maybe they really liked these games, too.

Finally, Miss Tina got on me and we did our work, then walked to the judges' arena. I watched one of the hats nod to me, but I waited to feel Miss Tina's command. She pressed me forward and I put my nose down and loped over the first poles. Then we jogged, then loped, then jogged again, to a place where I backed around a corner, and walked over a bridge. We jogged a little more, and finally arrived at the gate.

It took everything in me not to back up when she took hold of the rope. I was so excited, I may have backed up with my head a little too high. I was looking at the judges, trying to see if they liked looking at me. Suddenly, I felt her legs pushing me again, so I walked through the gate, then backed, and stopped. The gate was done and it was good. At least, I didn't move it.

It was over, then. Miss Tina patted my neck as we left the judges. That meant we did good.

MomToo joined us again, and we waited to hear names and numbers. This time I was fourth horse, which I remembered Bubba saying wasn't great but wasn't bad. Miss Tina and Auntie Niki started talking points again. I do not understand humans and their math. For horses, there are no numbers, no adding and subtracting. There is more, and there is less.

We walked back to the barn, but I did not get unsaddled. I was tied up and given a drink of water. Miss Tina didn't even take her shiny shirt and big hat off. After my drink, MomToo took me out again and we walked over to a different, empty arena.

I don't really understand a lot of what happened next. I wanted to be unsaddled and back in my stall, eating some hay. Instead, I was standing out in the sun while Auntie Niki went away, then came back with a piece of paper. Next, Miss Tina took the paper and went away. Then she came back and talked. Then she took me and walked over to a step, and got in my saddle again.

We walked into the empty arena and stood in the middle. I heard a big voice saying a bunch of stuff about a saddle and some farm and a sponsor, whatever that is. Then I heard a few words I knew.

"The 2007 Trail Futurity winner is My Flashy Investment, owned by Gayle Carline and shown by Tina Duree."

Humans outside the arena were making noises with their hands and someone was pointing a black box at us and making it go *click-click*. There was a shiny saddle next to me, and a big blue ribbon.

I could see MomToo at the fence, looking very happy. I had won.

I thought this meant I could go back to the barn now, but I didn't. Instead, Miss Tina rode me over to a little place with lots of plants, and straw, and spots like the numbers on my pads.

The shiny saddle was now in front of me. Everyone was there. MomToo, Auntie Niki, even Miz Cee, and the man and little dog who sometimes come with MomToo. They all stood next to me while another man with a big black box kept making *click-click* noises.

I wanted to eat the plants, or see if I could pick up the little dog, but Miss Tina wouldn't let me. She just kept saying, "Take the picture. I think he's had enough excitement."

She couldn't have been talking about me. I wasn't excited at all.

After forever, I got back to the barn. This time, I was unsaddled and the bands were taken out of my mane, so I knew I wouldn't be showing again.

"What happened?" Bubba asked.

"I let Miss Tina tell me when," I said.

"That's good. What horse were you?"

"Fourth."

"Hmm. First would have been better."

"Yes, but I won anyway."

"You won the class?"

I wasn't sure what he meant by this. "I don't know what a class is. All I know is that I went into an arena and a voice said I was the winner of the two sand seven trail futurity."

Bubba sounded pretty happy about the news. "That's great. Aren't you happy you won?"

"I'm happy I made MomToo happy." I stopped to think about how happy it made me. Apples and carrots make me happy. Running makes me feel good. Throwing things is fun. What did it feel like to be in the middle of an empty arena and have all the humans looking at me and making those slappy noises with their hands?

I nodded. "Yes. Yes, I'm happy I won."

After my win.
Miss Tina is in the saddle, MomToo is next to me, followed by her husband, Dale, Auntie Niki, and Miz Cee. The little dog is hiding behind the sign so I won't grab him.
(Photo by Don Trout.)

CHAPTER TWENTY-FIVE

After that show, things changed. For one thing, Miss Tina wasn't riding me as much, and MomToo started riding me again. For another thing, they started using a different bit in my mouth. I was used to wearing one of two things. Either I wore a smooth metal bit that bent in the middle and pulled at the sides of my mouth, called a snaffle, or I wore a bridle with only a hard loop on my nose that pulled my face down, called a bosal.

Now I was wearing a solid piece of metal in my mouth that pulled at my jaw, called a curb bit. None of these things bothered me. Miss Tina did not yank on the reins, or keep my head pulled down all the time. MomToo was a little more jerky with her hands, but she tried hard to give me my head, so I forgave her when she pulled too sharply.

We also stopped going to horse shows for a long time. Bubba went to another show, called a *World* show. I didn't get to talk to him as much as when we were traveling together, but he told me that the World is a very important show and you must be invited to it. That sounded like fun.

"We'll get Snoopy qualified for next year's World show," I heard Miss Tina tell MomToo one day. "I'll show him in the Junior Horse in February and you can start showing him in the Novice Amateur."

The weather got colder, especially at night, so we all wore two blankets. And the rain came. Lots and lots of rain. I like to play in the puddles, but I wasn't allowed to run around in them. Mostly, they'd put me on the hot walker and make me walk around in circles. After I had been around a few times, I would spend the rest of the time trying to get loose.

The hooks are not very tight, and I learned if I could reach them with my lips, I could pull my halter free. Then Auntie Niki learned if she put a hook with a clip on me, I couldn't unhook myself. Humans are really strict sometimes.

And Auntie Niki is really smart.

One day I was standing in the cross-ties, enjoying the sun and chewing on the chain. Wendy was standing next to me and a young girl was grooming her. The girl rubbed her withers, making Wendy stretch her neck out because it felt so good.

Suddenly I heard Rusty's voice. "So long, suckers."

Wendy and I looked up to see him being led toward the parking lot.

"Are you going to a show?" I asked.

"No, I'm going to a new home. I'm going to be a jumper." He seemed very excited.

The horses in the barn on the hill above us were jumpers. I used to watch them when I was little. Their stalls were at the bottom of my pen and I got to know a few of them. According to Mom, they were not Quarter horses, and I was not to talk to them, because they weren't very smart. I love Mom, but I may not be so smart, either, so I didn't see the harm.

It turns out most of them were pretty friendly, even with a young horse like me. They liked two things—treats, and fences. Horses can have several conversations about treats alone, so we always had plenty to discuss.

Still, I was sorry to see Rusty leave. He was my half-brother, and I liked him.

"Why can't he stay here and jump?"

Wendy snorted. "Because his owner sold him to a family who lives far away. They cannot keep him here and train him to jump."

"Why didn't his owner train him to jump?"

"I suppose she does not want to jump. She likes to do trail, like you. She has two horses, Bubba and Elliot, who do that now, so I guess she decided to let Rusty have the chance to do what he likes."

I remembered Bubba talking about his owner."Miz Cee owns Rusty?"

"Yes," Wendy said as she was being led to the arena.

So Miz Cee owned my best friend and my half-brother. It was certainly a small ranch.

At last, the rains stopped and it was sunny and warm every day. It felt good to be able to run and play again in the wood pen. I was kind of four years old by then. I heard MomToo explaining it. I was born in a month called April, but all Quarter horses have their birthdays in a month called January. I don't really know what months are, but she said it so often, I felt like I should know.

The best part was, I got to go to shows again with Bubba. It was just like before, except Auntie Niki didn't put the bands in my mane. A lady named Liz came around to the show and did it. Usually, Miz Cee would take Bubba out and Liz would band him, then they'd work their way to me.

Bubba told me that because I was four now, I was expected to act more like a grown-up horse and not move around and try to grab things. I tried really hard, although sometimes I forgot and Miz Cee would snap the lead rope. She and Liz talked a lot. Most of it was about horses and people I didn't know, but their constant voices were relaxing.

Miss Tina was still the only one riding me at the shows. It was just like the shows before, except I wore a different bit, and I always went into the arena twice now. Bubba said they were different classes. I still wasn't sure what a class was. All I knew was, I went into the arena once and saw the judges, then stood around the outside forever, and went into the arena again.

The first time in the arena, I would listen to Miss Tina really hard and put my feet over the poles without kicking them. By the second time in the arena, we were going over the same poles in the same direction, and I had waited forever to do the same thing again. It's hard to focus when you've done it all before. I wanted to look around at the judges and the humans and the plants.

Miss Tina always said the same thing after our second time. "He was so good in the Green, but he's bored by the time we get to the Junior."

I didn't know what green or junior was, but I wasn't bored. I just already knew what to do with my feet, so I wanted to think about something else.

MomToo still only rode me at home. We went over lots of poles in our arena. Miss Tina told us where to go and what to do. MomToo's seat was not as balanced as Miss Tina's, and her hand was not as soft on the reins. Sometimes, I understood where she wanted me to go and I went there. It made her happy.

Sometimes, I couldn't figure it out. Her body felt tense and I couldn't feel where her balance was, or her hand would be pulling me the wrong direction. Once that happened, we would spend the rest of our time together going over the same poles, until I was tired and she was sad.

One time, after a sad day's ride, I could feel her heart's heaviness as she led me back to my stall. She took my halter off and patted my neck. "How am I ever going to show you?" she asked me.

I wanted to tell her it was okay and that we would learn to understand each other. I reached over to try to make her feel better, but forgot what I was doing and grabbed her shirt.

She slapped me with the lead rope, and said, "And stop biting me!"

I felt bad. I liked being in the shows, and I knew MomToo wanted to be in them, too. Someday, she would be a better rider and I would be a better listener. In the meantime, I was a little happy that she didn't ride too well. I didn't want her to need a better horse.

CHAPTER TWENTY-SIX

Horses don't understand these things called calendars. We keep track of time in general by the sun and moon, but we've learned to understand how humans refer to it. One sunrise is a day. One moon's cycle is a month. We don't count the years. Humans do that for us.

On one bright morning, MomToo brought me a bunch of carrots and said, "Happy real birthday, Snoopy!"

Auntie Niki asked, "Is today his birthday?"

"April 28," MomToo replied.

I'm telling you this because MomToo tells everyone that it was two days after my fourth birthday that the bad thing happened.

The bad day started out as a good day. Finally, after forever, I heard that MomToo was going to ride me in a show. We were doing a little better, although I knew she didn't feel like we were going to do a very good job in the show arena.

"We've got to start somewhere," she told me.

On that day, MomToo got me out of my stall and brushed me, fast. She didn't spend her usual time with the curry and the hoof pick. She threw my saddle on and took me to the wood pen.

I didn't want to run much. She had to chase me and I could tell she wasn't happy about it. Everything she did was quick and not patient. After a little time in the wood pen, she brought me out, put my bridle on, and went to the arena.

I suppose I should have done what MomToo asked. She was riding me around and asked for the lope to my left. I was having a little problem getting started. She was a little stiff, although I could feel her balance okay. My left back leg felt a little funny. Instead of loping, I started to hop around.

"Take him back to the round pen," Miss Tina said. "He's still full of it."

"I had to chase him to get him to run at all," MomToo told her.

"Well, he's lazy and he's got your number. Have Niki help you."

I didn't know what number I had, but MomToo got off and led me back to the wood pen. Auntie Niki went in with us. Even though my leg still felt funny, I ran for Auntie Niki. When she says "run" you don't argue.

Now my leg started to hurt as I ran. Not bad, but it made me want to skip over that foot. It was okay. I had three more.

"Bring him down to the trot," I heard Auntie Niki say.

"Trot," MomToo told me. I trotted, but I still skipped over that leg. It didn't hurt bad, but it kind of pinched.

"Walk him," Auntie Niki said.

I walked. My leg still hurt. MomToo stopped me and led me out of the wood pen. She walked me back and forth by the barn. Auntie Niki stood there, nodding and talking. She called to Miss Tina, who watched me walk and trot.

Usually, I can tell when humans are happy or sad, but that day everyone felt funny, like they would like to be happy but they were afraid instead. I wondered what could make them afraid. I looked around, but there was nothing that scared me.

While the three of them talked about what to do, one of my favorite humans, Doctor Brigid came. She doesn't care if I try to chew her clothes. She feeds me cookies. When I bite, she blames it on my evil twin. "Snoopy doesn't bite," she says. "It's his evil twin."

I don't know what an evil twin is, but if he gets me cookies, I like him.

Doctor Brigid has many silver toys that I would like to play with, but she won't share them. She picked up my foot and used some of the toys on my hoof and ankle. Then she pushed on my leg with her hands. It was my back foot, but I could turn my head a little bit and watch.

Finally, I got another cookie.

"It might be an abscess," she said to MomToo. "It's not five o'clock yet, so the hospital is still on day rates. It might be the most expensive abscess you've treated, but I think you should take him down and have the foot X-rayed."

I heard all the words, but I didn't understand what she meant. What's a hospital, or an X-ray? I knew what an abscess was. That's what they called it when I was only a baby and my foot hurt when I walked. I stood in hot water and got scratched and rubbed by MomToo and Auntie Niki. The water was kind of icky, but the scratching made it okay.

Soon Auntie Niki led me into the moving box. I knew we weren't going to a show, but I liked it better when my friends came with me. This time I was alone.

We didn't go far. I didn't know where we were, but it was a big barn, bigger than the barn where I live. Some man led me into a stall with no shavings. There was a big silver box in the stall that I wanted to touch, but they wouldn't let me. Strange humans were picking up my foot and putting it right here and right there and if I moved it, they moved it back. I heard clicking noises like when I won the trail futurity.

A man in a white coat walked in and looked at a smaller box. He said his name was Dr. Klohnen, and he called to MomToo and pointed to the box and said things. He used funny words, so I couldn't understand him as well. There were words like, "See the white line... left hind sesamoid... fused... plate... screws... surgery."

I didn't know what anything meant, but I could see what they meant to MomToo. Her eyes looked kind of wide and she wasn't smiling. Her face looked kind of gray. I could feel her heart. It was afraid.

Poor MomToo.

They led me to a stall with weird shavings. It smelled funny, not like my stall. There was a nice lady in a white coat. She pinched my neck, then petted and rubbed me. It felt good. I tried to put her hand in my mouth, but she just laughed and petted me again.

I started to feel sleepy. I didn't try to bite the lady anymore. I closed my eyes and listened to my breath.

Two men came into the stall and ran a big strap under my tummy and hung the strap above my head. I could still walk, but I felt really light, and I couldn't lie down. It might have been scary to be trapped, except I was so sleepy I didn't care. I felt fine.

I called out to my neighbors. No one answered. Everyone seemed sleepy or sad.

I had a window, so I looked out. I could see horses down the hill jumping over big poles. It reminded me of when I was young and lived with Mom and Uncle Snowy. I used to watch the big horses jump over their poles. I also thought about Rusty and hoped he was having fun jumping. He sure had fun climbing things. I missed them all.

I'm glad they didn't teach me to jump over big poles. It looked like too much work.

My leg started to hurt a little more. I didn't have any food, so I closed my eyes and thought about the day and MomToo.

CHAPTER TWENTY-SEVEN

Pain woke me. Not my own pain, but the horse next to me. We don't talk about it when we hurt. Mom says it's because we don't want to attract anything that would kill us and eat us. But I felt my neighbor's pain even if he didn't cry out loud.

"What's wrong?" I asked.

"What isn't wrong?" I couldn't see him, but his voice sounded like he thought he was pretty special. "My legs hurt. My neck hurts. Those damnable humans have put me in a contraption that won't let me lie down."

So that's what I was in.

"I'm in a contraption, too. My leg hurts. Why are you here?"

He snorted at me. "Are you an idiot? Didn't you hear me? My legs and neck are hurt. Damnable humans tried to trick me into going into that dark, metal box. Horse trailers, hmpf. Deathtraps, I tell you. When I refused, they got rough with me and I fought them."

"You mean the big moving box? I like it. You get hay and watch trees go sideways. The floor goes up and down and—"

He stopped me. "You're a bigger idiot than I thought. That horrid thing cut my legs to ribbons. And then, with me screaming in pain, they actually forced me into it to bring me here. It was an outrage."

I suppose I should have been mad at him for calling me an idiot, but I like everyone. Being an idiot's not so bad. I could see he wasn't thinking so straight, hurting and all, so I thought I better leave him alone.

"Well, hope you feel better," I told him, and closed my eyes again.

I woke up a few more times during the night, but I still didn't have any food. I walked as far as my contraption would let me and looked out the window again. It was too dark to see if the horses were jumping over poles. I decided they probably didn't jump in the dark. I closed my eyes and slept a little, but my leg kind of hurt even without my weight on it.

It was light outside when the lady in the white coat came back. I was still a little sleepy, but I stretched my nose out to her. It made her smile. I like it when humans smile. She and the two men helped me down from my contraption and walked me outside. I looked behind and saw my foot was white and green. It was some kind of wrap. MomToo puts wraps on my front legs. She calls them polo wraps. This didn't look like a polo wrap, and I never wore anything on my back feet except shoes.

My leg felt stiff, but the lady walked slowly with me so I could do it. "Okay, Snoopy," she said and petted me while we walked. "Doctor Fischer is going to make you better."

As we passed my neighbor's stall, I looked in at him. He was a big gray horse with a long mane and tail. He had a strap like me and his legs were all wrapped with white and green, too. Even all bandaged, he looked like a very special horse.

"How are you this morning?" I asked him.

He snorted at me. "How do you think I am?"

I started to say I didn't know, because why would I ask, but the lady kept leading me until I couldn't see him anymore. I hoped he was better.

Soon we were in a funny stall that didn't have any shavings, but was soft on all the walls and floor. The two men came in to put another strap around my body. I was in another contraption.

I was going to have to thank the gray horse for the new word. Now I could tell my friends at home what they put me in.

Another lady came in with a little stick. I felt another pinch and then more rubbing. This time, I got very sleepy. The last time I felt this sleepy, I woke up very sore. Uncle Snowy the pony told me I had been gelded. I didn't know what that meant. I only knew I hurt.

As I lowered my head and closed my eyes, I hoped I wasn't getting gelded again.

It seemed that I woke up right away. I was still in the soft room, hanging by the contraption. I hung there forever, until I started stretching my legs and nodding my head. The lady in white came in.

"Ah, you are awake," she said. "Let us get you back to your stall."

The two men returned to unstrap me and the lady led me back. My foot felt even heavier, so I looked behind. I had a strange boot on my leg. It was white and covered me from my hock down, all around my hoof. I've never worn anything so heavy and it made me taller on one side. I had to swing my foot around to walk.

It made a weird sound as I returned to the stall. *Clop-clop-clop-thunk.* It was kind of funny sounding. *Clop-clop-clop-thunk.* I sometimes wish I was a human instead of a horse, so I could giggle. We can laugh out loud, but we can't just snicker a little.

I checked into my neighbor's stall again as we passed. He was still in his contraption and stood with his back to us, face in the corner. A lot of my friends do that. Usually they're napping. Sometimes they're thinking. I left him alone. He needed his rest.

Back in my own stall, there was still no food, but I was pretty sleepy, so it was okay. I had a drink of water, then I looked out the window. The horses were jumping their poles again. They were jumping so much and so high, it made me tired. I closed my eyes for a while. I guess being asleep all morning wears a guy out.

The next time I opened my eyes there was food in my stall. I buried my nose in the smell and took a big mouthful. It tasted different from my hay at home, but it was still good.

For a while, I didn't do anything except grab one bite after another. Then I slowed down and looked back out the window while I chewed. There weren't any horses in the arena, but there was one in a smaller pen, running around. He jumped and played, his tail over his back and snorting as he ran.

At home, we called that a turnout. It was a lot of fun, especially if we had been cooped up in a stall. I remembered how I once decided to jump out of the big turnout. Too bad I chickened out at the last minute and ended up hanging on the gate, half in and half out. I wasn't too scared. I knew someone would come and get me out of my mess. I was right, too. The ranch men ran right over and lifted me off the gate. They were a lot more excited about it than I was.

That was the last time I ever tried to jump over anything.

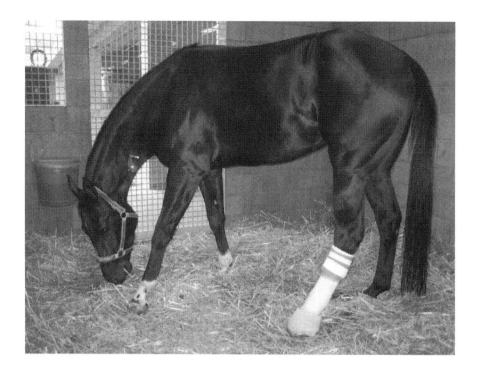

Me and my strange boot.

CHAPTER TWENTY-EIGHT

The lady in white came into my stall many times that day. Sometimes she came with another lady, sometimes a man. They rubbed and pinched and rubbed my neck, then put something into my bottom and petted me for a moment before removing it and making funny marks on boards, using little sticks.

Humans have a lot of different little sticks that all do different things.

I felt pretty sleepy, but I still tried to get hold of those little sticks to make my own marks. The lady in white laughed and rubbed my mouth. MomToo never rubbed my mouth. Auntie Niki and Miss Tina said it would make me want to bite more.

They're wrong. I don't want to bite. I just like to touch with my teeth. If it's chewy, I like to chew it. If it can be thrown, I like to throw it. Playing with my mouth doesn't make me want to touch humans more. It just doesn't make me want to touch them less.

After forever, a man came to clean my stall. At home, the two ranch men clean my stall. Not together. Some days it would be one and some days the other. They go down the line of stalls every day, talking and laughing. I like to hear them talk, although I can't always understand them. Their words are different than the ones MomToo uses, but they use MomToo's words when they talk to her. They are brothers, so mostly they talk about their family. Sometimes one of them sings.

Today I missed them. The man who cleaned my stall was nice, but he was a stranger. He did his job without talking or even singing. He cleaned everything up, then I saw him scratching on a little board with a stick outside my door. After he left, I tried to reach it, but I couldn't.

My stall had different bedding than at home. It was full of long skinny sticks that were kind of soft and kind of stiff, and not bad to chew. I think it was the kind of bed I was born in.

I heard my neighbor shuffling in his stall. It sounded like he could move around easier. Maybe he was in a better mood.

"How are you feeling today?" I asked.

For a long time, he said nothing, so I looked out my window again. The horses were in the arena, but they were going around the rail. No one was jumping. A man stood in the center and yelled at the horses and their humans. It looked like what Miss Tina called a group lesson. I like group lessons, but MomToo doesn't, mostly because I get very excited and want to play instead of learn.

It's hard to focus when you're surrounded by other horses and everyone's talking and so close you could scratch their withers if only their riders would let you. Our group lesson was usually in the morning when there were a lot of humans running in the street. Seeing the humans running made me want to run, too. They looked like they were having fun.

MomToo was not happy when I tried to play with the running humans.

All of a sudden, my neighbor said, "I guess I'm better. A little."

"That's good."

"How was your operation?" His words came out slowly and I didn't understand them all.

"What's an operation?"

"It's what they do here at the hospital." I heard him sigh. "Did they take you to a padded room and put you to sleep?"

I had to think about this. "Well, they took me to a room that was soft all over. Then, yes, I guess I fell asleep."

"When you woke up in the padded room, did you feel or look different?"

"Oh, yes, I have a big boot on my leg. It's very heavy and not like anything MomToo makes me wear."

His voice changed and became lower and softer. "Dear, dear, you have a cast on. Do you know what happened to your leg?"

"Not really. I was running in the wood pen, then my back leg started to hurt." I told him about Doctor Brigid and the stall with no bedding and the clicking noises, and the few words I heard the man in white say to MomToo.

"What's your name?" my neighbor asked me.

"My big name is My Flashy Investment, but everyone calls me Snoopy."

He snorted. "It fits. I'm Valentino. Snoopy, I'm afraid you've broken your leg."

As sleepy as I was, I admit my ears perked forward when I heard that. "I broke it? Does that mean it won't work anymore?"

He was quiet again for a moment. "For a rather simple horse, you have asked a hard question. Your leg may heal or it may not. If it heals, it may heal correctly, or you may always walk with a limp. If it heals correctly, you will still have work to do."

"Will it take a long time?"

"I do not know. You sound very young. That is good because you are healthy. But it is bad because you are impatient."

"I am four. How old are you?"

"Sixteen."

"Oh, wow, that's old. No wonder you were so cranky last night."

He made a chuffing sound. "Sixteen is not old. And of course I was cranky. I hurt everywhere. You will be cranky, too, when the medicine wears off and you start to feel what they did to your leg."

"They did something to my leg?"

I could hear the straps on his contraption jingling. I guess he wasn't unhooked yet. "Snoopy," he said at last. "Yes. That's what an operation is. They cut your leg open, probably put things in to straighten out the bone and keep it from moving around, then stapled the cut and put the big cast on to keep your leg completely stiff while it heals."

Now it was my turn to be quiet. He had said all this so very seriously, as if he was truly worried about my leg. I think when others are worried, they expect you to be worried, too. It was hard for me to be worried. Life is fun. I remembered he said either my leg would heal or it wouldn't.

I decided that it would.

CHAPTER TWENTY-NINE

My friend Valentino had stopped talking, so I watched the horses down the hill again. I was watching them jump when I heard a familiar noise, so I turned and looked out of my stall door. Auntie Niki and Miss Tina were outside.

Auntie Niki came in first. She patted the side of my neck. "How are you, Snoop?"

"Says on his chart he's got a little fever," Miss Tina said as she walked in. I felt her hand touch my hip, then run down my leg. "Cast looks good."

"They've still got him sedated," Auntie Niki said. "He's not very chewy."

I don't know what sedated meant, but she was right. I didn't really feel like putting anything in my mouth that wasn't food. Auntie Niki never let me push my nose against her, but today she did. She scratched my face between my eyes. It felt good.

"It'll probably be at least a week before he comes home," Miss Tina said. "I'll have the guys prep a stall. He'll have to be on straw until the cast comes off."

Straw. So that's what the long, sticky bedding was.

They walked back toward the door. I swung my leg around and faced them.

Miss Tina pointed at my cast. "Poor guy. Hope that doesn't have to stay on long. I'd hate to have him founder."

"See you tomorrow, Snoopy," Auntie Niki said and they left.

"Valentino?" I had questions, and he seemed like a smart horse. I had to call him a couple of times. He was pretty cranky by the time he answered.

"What?"

"Miss Tina and Auntie Niki said things I don't understand."

"What else is new?"

"Nothing's new. You've only been asleep a little while. The horses down the hill are still jumping—"

"Never mind, Snoopy. What didn't you understand?"

"Auntie Niki said I'd been, um, es-dated."

"What?" I could hear him shake his mane and snort. "You must mean sedated. It means you were given medicine to make you calm and even sleepy."

"Oh. And Miss Tina said she hoped I didn't founder."

Valentino was very quiet for a while. Then he spoke. "That is a serious fear, Snoopy. We need to keep the blood flowing in our legs, up to our heart and down to our hooves. If it doesn't keep flowing and feeding our feet, they begin to hurt. The wall that supports our hoof starts to decay."

"Then what happens?"

"Eventually the bones fall through the hoof. If you have a human who loves you, they have you put down before that happens. It is excruciating—I'm sorry—it is very painful."

I thought about Uno. Holly had said his leg was hurting and the bones would soon go down through his hoof. She said there was pain that would heal and there was forever pain. I shared this with Valentino.

"Could that thing, founder, happen to me?"

He shuffled around in his stall. "It could happen to either of us."

"But maybe not, right?"

"Right. Maybe not." He didn't sound like he believed in maybe.

"Right. It won't happen to me. Or to you."

"If you say so." Valentino chuffed a little. "I'm curious. With a name like My Flashy Investment, how did you get nicknamed Snoopy?"

"I'm not sure. Mom said I was named Snoopy before I was born. She was at a horse show and I was growing in her tummy. MomToo said I was the size of a beagle, whatever that is. Then Auntie Niki started calling me Baby Snoopy. I don't know why."

"I don't get it, either, but it is a good name for you. You are very inquisitive."

I wasn't sure what inquisitive meant, so I asked him, "Is Valentino your only name, or do you have more?"

"I believe it is all I need. I am an Andalusian of very old breeding. My sires and dams can be traced back to the Middle Ages, when we were warriors on men's battlefields. I myself have sired twenty foals and I am only sixteen. I was on my way to a new owner when I had my unfortunate accident."

"You're such a smart horse. I only know my mom and dad's names. Oh, and one grandfather."

"You are a Quarter horse, yes?"

"Yes."

"I hope I am not too impolite, but your breed does not have the kind of history as my own. You were born of this land, which is very young compared to where I come from. I would not expect much history from you. No offense."

"It's okay. Mom's the one who remembers stuff. I forget a lot. She told me I wasn't an old spirit, like her. My spirit is brand new."

"For a Quarter horse, your mother is wise. It's too bad I can't meet her. Is she still at the place where you were born?"

"Sure. I still live there, too."

"Amazing! Her human kept you, too?"

"MomToo? Well, sure. She rides me."

"Snoopy, you are a lucky horse. I myself had passed through two owners by the time I was your age. I'm now on my fourth."

"Is that bad?"

"No, they have all been nice humans, even if they weren't always wise. It's just hard to say goodbye, go to a new home, make new friends. I guess change comes to everyone."

He was quiet again. I guess he was thinking about everyone he said goodbye to, and I started thinking about Uncle Snowy, and Johnny and Tucker. Uncle Snowy was still in the pen where I used to be, but Johnny went away one day in the moving box, and Tucker went to a horse show with me, then went home with someone else.

I did miss them, but I meet so many new friends, it makes it all okay. Like Valentino. I only understood half of what he was saying, but he had a pretty way of talking.

Soon I heard another kind of noise outside my stall. It sounded like the cart at home, the one that brings my hay. It took forever, but finally I watched a man walk toward my door with something green in his hand. It was a whole flake of hay for me. I hadn't had anything to eat in forever, since the last time.

I was so hungry, I might have tried to eat the lady in white.

As I ate, she came into my stall with a man, who put my halter on and held my lead rope while I ate. She looked at my leg, in its cast, as Valentino had called it, then stuck something into my bottom again, and rubbed my chest with a silver toy that plugged her ears and scratched on the board with the little stick. While she worked, she talked to the young man, who held my lead rope.

"I'd like to see his temperature come down. It isn't a high fever, but it's not normal yet. Everything else looks good."

I didn't know what a temperature or a fever was, but I'm pretty sure no one's ever called me normal. At some point, I looked over at the man. He was looking at the lady, so I grabbed his shirt with my teeth. He yelled and the lady laughed.

Even with a temperature, I liked hearing that.

They left, so I went back to my hay. I was almost done when I heard a familiar voice.

"There's my Snoop Dog." It was MomToo.

I looked over at her, but didn't turn right away. It was becoming harder and harder to swing my leg around.

"Look at your cast," she said. "You've got a Franken-Foot now, huh?" Then she took a little soft curry out of her pocket and started to massage me. It felt good, so I nibbled on my food as she worked.

"You're kind of a mess." She rubbed and brushed. "Feels like you got a little sweaty, you're all crusty."

I continued to eat.

"Wish I knew how this happened, Snoop. You were just running. You weren't doing anything weird. Just running." She kept rubbing and brushing. I thought it felt like she was sad and maybe a little afraid, then she told me, "But it's going to be okay. You'll probably be home in a week or so, the cast will come off in a couple of months, and then... something."

I love MomToo, almost as much as Mom. Mom tries really hard to be calm, even though she would rather be afraid of everything. She taught me to be calm, too, and accept things. I could see how hard she had to work at it. MomToo always thinks everything's going to be okay. If she works at thinking that way, it never shows. Nothing's a big deal to her. It can all be fixed.

With two moms like that, what have I got to worry about?

After she had rubbed me down all over and my skin felt like I'd had a good day of scratching on a post, she hugged my neck. "I gotta go now, but I'll be back tomorrow to see you."

She left and my food was gone, so there was nothing else to do except watch the jumping horses. The man was in the arena with them again, talking. There were four horses, three chestnuts and a bay. Three of the horses were on the rail, working, while the fourth horse jumped poles in the middle.

MomToo doesn't like to ride me on the rail, but I hear Auntie Niki yell at her to go there. It doesn't matter to me whether I'm on the rail or not. I just don't like to go around the same place too often. I like to have fun.

After talking to Valentino, I missed having fun, and I even missed the rail.

CHAPTER THIRTY

After a lot of days, I began to think I would stay at the hospital forever. I had to stand in my stall and couldn't go outside. There was a small patch of grass out of my stall door where they walked other horses and I wanted so much to be walked around in the fresh air, but no one would take me out.

Every day was the same and it was hard to find something new to interest me. The lady in white stopped pinching me, but she still put that thing in my bottom and scratched on the little board with her stick. She looked at my cast and rubbed around the top of it. The stranger cleaned my stall and fed me every day. And from my window I watched the horses jump in the arena below.

Doctor Brigid came sometimes and gave me cookies. She would look at the board outside, then come in and pet me. She also checked my legs. It seemed like everybody wanted to look at my cast, except maybe MomToo.

She came most days, too, but she didn't look at the board or my cast. She brought a curry out of her pocket and gave me a good rub and scratch. I looked forward that. My skin felt so itchy, it was good to be scratched and rubbed all over. Sometimes she brought a carrot. That was even better.

I wish she could have curried my cast. My leg was starting to itch. It kind of ached, too, and my back was kind of sore from lifting it around. I could see why Valentino was so cranky. It wasn't a bad pain, but the little hurt made me feel so tired.

"Valentino," I called to him one day when I heard him walking around. "Are you out of your contraption?"

"Yes, they've finally let me walk on my own, although it's not as wonderful as I thought it would be. My legs are still sore, and now they have to bear my entire weight. It's harder to lie down and get up, because they hurt. Of course, I'd rather be free than tied up like that."

"I'm sorry you hurt. I hope you get better."

As always, he was quiet for a while before he spoke again. It seemed like Valentino always thought about what he was going to say before he said it. "Snoopy, I must apologize. The day you came in I was in a lot of pain. I was rude to you, when you were just trying to make a friend."

"Oh, that's okay. I know I'm not a smart horse. Sometimes other horses call me names, because I do silly things. Even MomToo calls me a bonehead, whatever that is. Maybe I could have been smarter, but I like being friendly best."

I heard him laugh a little. "Friendly is good."

"Valentino, I was curious. It sounds like you've been in the moving box before. Why did you fight it so much and get hurt that day?"

"My previous owner was a nice woman, but there was much she didn't know about horses, and especially stallions. I was used to walking into the horse trailer and being tied, loosely, where I could eat my hay from a bag at my nose. The first time she loaded me, she did not tie me, nor did she tie the gelding next to me. Not only did I feel anxious, to be loose in the trailer, but the gelding reached across to my hay and we fought. She had to pull over and break us up. I know it frightened her.

"After that, she tied me in the trailer so tightly that I could not reach more than the top portion of my food. It was an endlessly long ride, during which I could smell and see my hay, but could not eat it. I'm afraid I was unhappy by the time we arrived and I came out of the trailer in a bad mood.

"Over time, she became more and more afraid of me, even though I am considered a gentleman among studs. Rather than working with an expert to learn how to handle me, she sold me to the man who owns me now.

"He is a nice man, but not an affectionate one and demands rather than asks me to do things. Recently, a woman came and looked at me. We spent some time together, working on the ground first, then she rode me. I could tell from the moment she looked me in the eye that she understood me, so I was excited when I heard she was going to buy me.

"But I am still very cautious about going into the trailer. I'd rather walk in by myself, slowly, once I'm satisfied that it is safe. When my current owner started slapping me with the lead rope I got mad. When his helper hit my rump with the rake, I decided to give them both a fight."

"I suppose it would have been easier to do what he said," I told him.

"Well, of course, if I had it to do again—" He stopped for a moment. "No, I was so angry, I don't exactly regret acting up. I only regret I was careless and got injured. Haven't you ever been that angry?"

I thought about it for a while. "No. Can't say anybody's ever made me mad at all."

"Never? No one's ever made you pin your ears and take a swipe at them?"

"No. I love Mom and could never be mad at her, my humans are good, and the other horses I've stayed with were there to teach me stuff. I guess I'd rather be happy."

"Snoopy, you are a wonder."

While we were talking, I heard someone come down the walk toward my stall. It was MomToo. She came in, petted my neck, then took out her curry.

"I think you're coming home this week," she said. "Your temperature is normal now. It has to stay that way for a couple of days."

She continued to talk as she rubbed. "I know it's been hard to stay cooped up in this stall. You're used to getting out. I'm afraid you're going to have to stay in your stall at home, too. But at least you'll have a door you can hang your head over, so you can see more of the outside."

The rubbing felt extra good today, especially on my hips. They were sore from moving the cast on my leg. She could have rubbed there forever, but she didn't. She stopped after a while.

"I gotta go now, but hopefully the next time I see you, it will be back at home."

She left and I was alone again. I turned to the window and watched the horses. One was in the arena, jumping the poles. Another was in the turnout, shaking his head and galloping big circles. So far I hadn't thought too much about going home. I had been at the hospital for such a long time, I stopped thinking about it. It made me sad to miss my old stall.

Now I wanted to go. I wanted to go in the wood pen and gallop and shake my head. I wanted to go out to the arena and walk over my poles on the ground. I would miss Valentino, but I didn't want to be here anymore.

CHAPTER THIRTY-ONE

A couple of days later, after I had eaten and watched the man clean my stall, the lady in white came in and looked at my leg and stuck that little stick in my bottom. She smiled and patted my neck. I tried to chew on her coat, but she put her hands on my mouth and rubbed my lips.

"Looks like you can go home today, Snoopy," she said, and left.

Home at last. I was so happy to hear that. "Valentino, did you hear the lady? I'm going home."

"I heard. That's good news."

"I'll miss you."

"I'll miss you, too, Snoopy. For a simple horse, you have been a pleasant neighbor."

"When are you going home?"

"I don't know. My owner hasn't visited me and the doctor does not talk when she is examining me."

This surprised me, so much that I blurted out, "Your owner hasn't visited? Sorry, was that a bad thing to say?"

"No. You are a very lucky horse, Snoopy. You have been born into a family, more than most horses these days. Your owner loves you. I can tell by the way she comes into your stall and talks to you about her day. Even your trainers come to visit. Cherish your life, and get well. You are blessed."

They were such nice things for him to say, I didn't really know how to answer. I usually don't mind sounding stupid. But he made me want to sound smarter.

"Thank you. I hope you get better and go home soon, too."

"I'm sure I will. I feel myself getting stronger every day."

He didn't say anything more, so I turned and watched the horses jumping. I hadn't been as happy watching them for a while, because I wanted to be out of my stall, too. Today, it was fun again, knowing I was going home.

The sun was very high when Miss Tina walked in with my lead rope. "Come on, Snoopy, let's go home."

We walked slowly down the barn aisle. I had plenty of time to say goodbye to my friend. It took us forever to go around the corner, where I saw the big moving box. I was so happy, I reached for Miss Tina's sleeve, but she tapped me on the nose with the rope.

Walking up the ramp was a lot different with my cast. It was hard to get my foot underneath me so I had to go faster with my other back foot and kind of hop up to the box. Miss Tina kept the rope very loose and let me pick my way. Once I was inside, she tied me to the wall and closed the door.

The box only moved a little way, then stopped. I looked out of the window and saw our barns. I was home. At first, I thought I'd have to back down the ramp, which might be hard to do with my cast. But Miss Tina untied my rope and turned me around, real slow, so I could walk forward.

It felt good to be back at my own ranch. Miss Tina led me into the first barn, to a stall with straw in it. MomToo was there, watching. If I could have, I would have smiled like she did.

I walked around in my new stall once, just to make sure everything was the same as the other barn where I lived before, like the water and the food. Then I stuck my head over the door and tried to chew on MomToo. She smacked my nose, but I think she was happy.

There were different horses in this barn. Betty, a buckskin mare, was next to me. A black mare named Lulu was in the corner. Most of the horses were mares here, except for me and Jet. I had met him at the horse show forever ago. He wasn't very friendly then. I tried to talk to him but he wasn't friendly now, either. He was too busy talking to the mares.

"Hey, Jet, I was at the hospital, but now I'm home," I told him.

"So what?" He tossed his head up and down and made funny noises with his lips.

"That's cool, how do you do that?" I nodded really fast and let my mouth flap. It sounded funny, so I did it again.

"Whatever," he said, then called to Betty. "Hey, baby, you are looking fine today."

Betty didn't answer him. I heard her walk to the corner of her stall and stand quietly.

I missed Bubba, and Valentino, and even cranky BuddyTwo, who at least talked to me. Just then, a familiar face looked out of the stall across from mine.

"How are you feeling?" It was Mom.

I was so happy to see her, I forgot all about everyone else. "Mom, I'm glad you're here. You won't believe what happened, or where I've been."

"I know a lot of it," she said. "Lulu was there when you went to the hospital. And Gayle has told me what happened. How is your leg?"

"It itches, and it hurts a little. Mostly, it's heavy and I have to drag it around. My back is tired."

"I think itching might be good. I've heard it means the break is healing. Once it's healed, they will take the cast off and you won't have to drag your foot around anymore. Were you very bored in the hospital? You were there for a long time."

"Yes, but I tried not to be bored. I met a stallion named Valentino, and he was nice to talk to. He said he'd like to meet you sometime."

Mom snorted. "I'm sure he would."

"Stallion?" Jet shook his head around. "Where's the stallion? This is my barn."

"Ignore him," Mom said. "He thinks he's the leader and we're all part of his herd."

Soon, everyone in the barn was quiet, so I ate some of my food. It tasted like the food I ate when I was a baby. That food helped me grow. Maybe now it would help me heal.

It was starting to get hard to tell if my leg hurt or not. There was a small pain that went up into my hips and down my back. My other three legs were working more to keep the weight off the broken one, so they were aching. Lying down made them hurt less, but getting back up wasn't easy.

I ate my food and thought about pain that heals and forever pain. I wanted this to be the pain that heals, and hoped MomToo didn't think it was forever pain. My brand new spirit wasn't ready to go looking for the Clover Fields.

CHAPTER THIRTY-TWO

I was happy to be home, but it wasn't as nice as I thought it would be. I wanted to be in my old stall, near Bubba. The horses in this barn didn't have much to say, and after a while, even Mom told me I talked too much. I could hang my head over my metal door, which was a good thing. My stall was smaller than the one at the hospital, so there wasn't a lot of room for me to walk around.

The next afternoon, it was warm and I was sleepy, so I laid down for a nap. The straw was soft. I dreamed of running in the wood pen.

A noise woke me. It was MomToo.

"Aw, are you getting a nap?" Her voice was soft, but I heard it.

Maybe she had treats for me. I stretched my legs out, including the one with the cast, then I stood up. That's when I felt a tug. I couldn't get my leg on the ground. I looked behind me. MomToo was tugging at the clippie on the gate, saying very bad words. I could feel her fear. Looking at what scared her, I saw my cast was stuck under the stall door.

I wasn't afraid. I just pulled until my cast wasn't stuck. The door got a little bent, but it was all okay. It kind of hurt to use my leg that much, so I limped over to get a drink of water. That made MomToo even more frightened. She took out her little talking toy and started pressing on it and holding it to her ear.

She did this a bunch of times, until she finally said, "Doctor Brigid, it's Gayle. I'm here alone at the ranch and Snoopy got his cast stuck in his stall door. He got it free but he's limping and the hospital won't answer and everyone's at lunch and I'm hoping he didn't re-break anything." Her voice sounded pretty wobbly by the time she said a bunch of numbers and pressed another button.

Had I broken my leg again? I took a couple of steps. It was a little sore from pulling on it, but nothing hurt like before it was in the cast.

MomToo's toy made noises and she put it to her ear again. She said a few words, then pressed the button. I could feel her trying not to be afraid for me. Her eyes got watery, but she wiped them.

After a while, Doctor Brigid came into the barn. MomToo explained what happened again, and Doctor Brigid had her put my halter on and lead me out of the stall. It felt good to be outside, even if I did have to lift the cast really high to get it out of the stall door.

First, Doctor Brigid looked at my leg and felt around in my cast. After that, we walked to one end of the barn, then turned around very slow, and walked to the other end. Then Doctor Brigid put one of those sticks in my bottom, and waited for it to make a noise. It beeped, and she took it out and looked at it.

"His temperature is normal. He is limping a little, but it's not bad, and his cast didn't crack, or rub on his leg. Let's monitor him to make certain." She pointed to my door. "And let's get rid of this door and use the sliding one instead. It goes all the way to the ground."

MomToo helped me get back into the stall. I wasn't sure what would have happened if Doctor Brigid didn't like my cast or my temperature, but I was glad to stay home. MomToo closed my metal door, then closed the heavy sliding door, too. That made me unhappy. The sliding door had bars on it, so I couldn't hang my head outside. With a small stall, I really liked looking out at the world.

At least, I could feel the fear wash away from her and she was happy again, which was good.

The ranch men came later in the day and took the metal door off. MomToo put a toy in my stall for me to play with. It was a big rubber ball with a handle. I stepped on it and made it all flat. Then I looked out through the bars, wondering when this would all be over.

Breaking your leg was no fun.

The best parts of my day became when the ranch men brought food and when they came to clean my stall. I started to yell for them every time I saw the wheeled bucket. I knew they'd open my stall door and prop it in the middle while they cleaned. That meant I could hang my head outside for a little while and get some fresh air.

Even here at home Miss Tina or Auntie Niki kept coming into my stall and putting a stick in my bottom. It became their regular greeting. "Hi, Snoop, I'm here to take your temperature."

MomToo just came in to curry and brush me and tell me how long before my cast came off. I liked having her talk to me.

CHAPTER THIRTY-THREE

One morning, I woke up feeling kind of bad. My leg was hurting. I was getting used to it aching, but this was a different kind of pain, from my skin. My body also felt too warm. I felt groggy and sad and plain old icky.

Miss Tina greeted me with my temperature, as usual. Then she felt around my cast. She took out her little talking toy, pushed buttons, and talked. After a while, she led me out of my stall and to the big moving box. We moved a little, then stopped.

We were back at the hospital.

From listening to Miss Tina and the humans in white coats, I had a fever and a sore where the cast rubbed. I didn't think it was so bad, but they were all worried about something called an infection. All I knew was, I was led to the back of the hospital, to a different stall. This time, I couldn't see the horses jumping. All I saw was a corral and stacks of hay from my window. I did see the patch of grass outside my door, and sometimes horses passing by.

I wondered if Valentino was still there. I called out to him, but he didn't answer. A strange voice in the stall next to me asked who I was looking for.

"My friend, Valentino. He was a…" I couldn't remember what he called himself, so I just said, "He was a big gray stallion."

"Ah, yes, I saw him. They walked him around the courtyard every day." The voice sounded very tired. "But I haven't seen him for a while."

"Oh, then maybe he went home." I was disappointed that my friend was gone, but happy to know he'd gone back to his owner.

"Maybe. Or maybe he went with the knacker."

"What's a knacker?"

"The man who carries the body away, after a horse dies."

"Oh. At my ranch, they call that the teal truck." This thought had not occurred to me. Valentino dead? No, it must not be. He was getting stronger, not weaker. I decided he had gone home.

"That's probably where he went," the voice continued. "He wasn't walking so good."

"He was injured pretty bad," I said. "But when I left him, he had already gotten much better." I thought about what Valentino said about my operation. "It may take a long time for him to heal. Just because he wasn't walking so good doesn't mean it was a forever pain."

"What does having forever pain matter? Humans are impatient. They don't want to wait until you get better. If you're not better now, they'd rather get rid of you and get another horse."

"But my human is waiting for me to get better. They gave me an operation and put a cast on my foot to help me."

He was silent for a moment and I thought maybe I had convinced him. Then he said, "They may be willing to try, but once that cast comes off, if you don't heal right away, it'll be off to the knacker, I guarantee. They'll tell you how it's better for you, how you won't be in pain and all that junk. But really, it's because you're broken. No one wants to feed and stable a broken horse when they can get rid of you and get a new one."

This stranger sounded very sad about the world. My fever was making me feel sad anyway, and he was making me feel worse. I was also now a little worried that MomToo would decide I had forever pain when all I had is pain that heals. I didn't want to talk to him anymore even though I would like to have someone to talk to. I thought about BuddyTwo.

"You sound like you've never been loved," I told him.

He didn't answer.

This time, the hospital was scary. My leg was hurting on the inside and outside, and I felt all hot and sick. They put holes in my cast so it didn't hurt the outside, and came in and pinched my neck with their little sticks. The lady in white came in many times every day to put the other stick in my bottom and make scratches on the board.

I just wanted to go home.

My neighbor stayed pretty quiet. I didn't even know his name. After our first talk, I did not want to bother him again. He was so sad and angry, and I didn't want to be sad and angry with him. Mostly, our talk made me scared, and I didn't want to be afraid.

CHAPTER THIRTY-FOUR

One morning, I heard his stall door open and the sounds of hooves on hard ground. I looked out my door to see if I could see him. He was being led around the yard. He was a tall, thin brown horse. I don't think I've ever seen a horse so skinny. I could see all of his bones, and he walked slow, like his feet were sore. His face was very long, and there was something about his eyes. As he turned, he looked at me. I tried to meet his stare, but had to turn away. There was something so very unhappy about his eyes, it frightened me.

I went back into the corner of my stall and stared out the window. Maybe they'd put a horse in the pen next to the hay and I could talk to someone happier. Soon, I heard my neighbor come back.

"So you're the new kid," he said. "I saw you at the door."

"My name is Snoopy. What's yours?"

"What does it matter?"

"I guess it doesn't. I just like to be friendly."

"Friendly." He said it like a mouthful of bad hay.

I kept looking out the window, wishing for something fun to happen. After forever, I heard my neighbor again.

"Kid Galahad."

"Excuse me?" I said.

"My name. It's Kid Galahad."

"Is that your show name? Or what your owner calls you?"

"It's my only name. I'm a race horse. Or at least, I was."

I had only met one race horse on our ranch. One of the horses in the jumper barn told me he had been a race horse but he didn't like it. His name was Topper. They tried to make him run as fast as he could in a big circle to the left, with other horses.

"It's dangerous out there on the track," he had told me. "There are too many horses running together, and my rider was always trying to get me to pass them, always where I would get pushed. I much prefer being a jumper. It's kind of hard, but I'm the only one in the arena when I do it, and I love my owner. She is the kindest human I've ever known."

"Were you in a lot of races?" I asked Kid Galahad.

"Too many. I started out winning, or nearly winning. Then I went to just nearly winning. Nearly winning isn't good enough for humans. Out of eight or nine horses, I only let three or four get ahead of me. I was never last. But they didn't like it. I was sold at auction."

"What's auction?"

"It's a horrible, noisy, smelly place where they bring you into a pen and walk you around for humans to see. There is an awful racket, where one human is talking fast and a bunch of other humans are yelling at him. Then you hear a strong knock and the word 'Sold'. You are led out of the pen and they hand you over to a stranger."

"Was your stranger nice?"

"No. She was a stupid woman who had never owned a horse. She bought me because I was cheap and gave me to her grandson. He told me he didn't even want a horse, much less me. He tried to ride me a couple of times, but I couldn't figure out what he wanted. I've been trained to run on a track. My riders kneel over my withers and urge me forward. They pull back on my mouth to make me run faster, and relax the reins to make me stop."

"Wow. That's not what I was taught."

"It is not the way horses are taught to be ridden anywhere else but the racetrack. I know this. But without being trained a different way, I don't know how to be ridden anywhere else but the track."

"Did the grandson teach you?"

"Of course not. He didn't know. He barely knew how to put the saddle on, and he could not stay balanced on my back. He just dug his legs into my sides and pulled my head back. When he pulled on the reins, I thought he wanted me to run, so I did. He started screaming, which made me run faster. Then he fell off and blamed me for it. He tried again, but he wasn't any better.

"So they just left me in a stall. One day, I only got breakfast and no dinner. That went on for a while, until I stopped getting breakfast, too. My feet started to hurt. They had left my old shoes on, and my hooves were growing and pushing them sideways on my feet. I began to look for the knacker every day. At first, I looked because I was frightened. Then I started to look because it would be a relief to leave this horrid place and go to the Clover Fields, if I was lucky enough to get there."

Lucky enough? "Why do you need to be lucky to go to the Clover Fields?"

"Not every horse goes, you know. Only the ones who've been good and useful, or the ones who have very old spirits and have crossed over many times."

Uncle Snowy didn't tell me this part. "Where do the rest of them go?"

"Nowhere. They just... stop being." I heard him breathe out a little. "I'll probably stop being. My spirit is probably a new one, and even though I haven't been a bad horse, I haven't been particularly good, or useful."

This talk was making me even more sad and scared. "If you're here in the hospital, it must be because your owner thinks you'll get better."

"Pfft. I was taken away from that owner by a man in a uniform and brought here. They've trimmed my feet, and they've given me hay and water. If I survive, they'll try to find a better home for me. But I won't survive. It's too late."

"No, Kid Galahad." I couldn't let him think this. "Keep eating and drinking and walking around your stall. Build up your strength. They would not have brought you here unless they wanted you to live. You need to try for the man in the uniform and the humans here. They care about you."

"No one cares about me," he said. "And I don't care about them."

I didn't know how to make him believe in the humans here who were helping us both. So I said nothing and went back to watching out the window. Dinner came, as well as the lady in white, who checked me over as usual. I grabbed at her coat and she laughed and pushed my mouth away.

"You are so mouthy, Snoopy," she told me. "But your temperature is better, and your sore is healing nicely. I think maybe tomorrow you can go back home."

That made me happy, and I went to sleep and dreamed of running around in the wood pen. I had only slept a little bit when I heard a noise that woke me. It was still dark, but the moon was very bright and shone into my window.

"Goodbye, Snoopy." It was Kid Galahad.

And then I heard a loud thumping sound, and I knew it was him, falling to the floor.

"Kid Galahad." I cried out so hard my own scream hurt my ears. "Kid Galahad, get up."

In a little while, I heard human feet, and the voice of one of the men who worked here. "Snoopy, what are you screaming about?"

I think he was coming to my stall, but I heard him stop and enter the stall next to mine. There were some scuffling noises, and then his voice again.

"Doctor Pollard, this is Joe. The rescue you brought in is down... his breathing is shallow... okay."

Joe stayed with my neighbor until I heard feet again, coming into the next stall, and Doctor Pollard's voice.

"I didn't know if we had much of a chance with him, but I was hoping. What a shame."

They didn't say anything else for a while, then I heard some words about the truck coming tomorrow morning. Kid Galahad was right. The knacker was coming for him.

CHAPTER THIRTY-FIVE

It was a bad night. I couldn't sleep, knowing Kid Galahad was in the next stall, lying still forever. No one had told him goodbye, like MomToo had told Uno and Holly. He hadn't been loved. This was hard for me to believe. All the horses I knew there were loved. At least I thought they were. How could there be a horse with no human to love him?

I also kept thinking about what Kid Galahad said about only going to the Clover Fields if you have been good and useful, or an old spirit who has been there many times. Mom said my spirit was new, so that would not get me to the fields. I wondered if winning the futurity made me useful to MomToo. Did I have to be useful to a lot of humans, or was one enough?

Being good was a challenge. I *tried* not to grab things. I *tried* not to run into other horses and bite them on the bottom. I *tried* to be a good horse. I wondered if you got in if you tried really hard, even if you didn't succeed all the time.

The sun came up and the man came in to give me food. I ate a little of it, but it was hard to do. The other stall had begun to smell bad. This must be what death smelled like. After forever, I heard a familiar roar outside my window. I looked up to see the truck with the walls—the one Uncle Snowy had called the teal truck.

Lots of humans walked past my door, dragging a big cloth, bigger than anything MomToo used on my face. They opened my neighbor's door and I heard strange sounds, thumping and whooshing, and footsteps. Then I heard a steady shushing noise. I looked out my door to see something awful.

Kid Galahad was in the middle of the cloth and there were men dragging the cloth past me toward the teal truck. He was on his side, mostly, and his legs stuck out so the men had to keep out of their way while they pulled on the cloth. His eyes were open and empty.

I turned away and did not see them put him on the truck. After forever, the truck went away. So did the bad smell. I started eating again. The woman in the white coat came in and looked me over, making her usual scratches on her board.

"You're doing very well, Snoopy," she told me. "Looks like you can go home today."

I was glad. The humans were nice, but I never wanted to be in this place again.

CHAPTER THIRTY-SIX

When Miss Tina picked me up that day, I wanted to leap into the trailer. She and my heavy cast wouldn't let me, so I walked. As we went to the front of the hospital, there was another, small trailer there. I saw a familiar face standing at the end of the trailer, looking inside.

"Valentino," I called out to him. "You're going home?"

"Why, hello Snoopy. Yes, I am finally well enough." He shook his head at the tall blonde woman holding his lead rope and clucking softly. "My new owner knows how to treat me. She and I will get along well. Take care and be a good horse."

I watched him step up and disappear into the dark trailer.

My heart was still full of sadness from my night with Kid Galahad, but at least he was wrong about my friend. Valentino was going to be fine.

At my home, Miss Tina led me back to the stall with straw across from Mom. It felt good to be at the ranch again. MomToo hung a toy in my stall that I could eat. It was sweet and I had to chase it around a little with my mouth to get hold of it.

It was a fun game and I ate all the sweet part as fast as I could.

"Snoopy." MomToo was in the barn, looking at me through the stall door. "You were supposed to lick that, not eat it."

I don't know why she would give me something to lick. I don't think I've ever licked anything that I didn't bite.

"Oh, well, I'm so glad you're home. Now you need to get better."

I wasn't sure what she meant by getting better, but I was glad to be home, too.

It was hard to be a good horse now. I stayed in my stall forever, and it wasn't easy finding interesting things to look at or touch. The ranch men came every day and fed me and cleaned the straw. I was so happy to see them, I wanted to get near them to rub my muzzle on them, but they pushed me away. Miss Tina came every day, too. She took my temperature and looked at my cast and my sore. I tried to grab things out of her hand, just to play with her, but she spanked me a little.

Still, she looked happy to see me.

MomToo came to visit a lot, too. Sometimes she had a curry and would give me a nice scratching. Sometimes she also had a bucket of water and a towel, and would wipe me down. This felt really good on a hot day. All the time, she talked to me.

"I'm so sorry you have to stand in here, Snoopy. You are so young, you should be able to run and play. But your leg is getting better, and soon the cast will come off and you can start exercising it. It's all going to be okay, you'll see."

I wasn't really sure of what she was saying about the cast and exercise, but I could feel her telling me that I would not die and go to the teal truck and on to the Clover Fields.

She made me feel good.

CHAPTER THIRTY-SEVEN

Just when I thought I would never leave my stall again, Miss Tina led me out one morning into the moving box. When we only moved a little, I knew we were back at the hospital. I didn't understand why we would be here. I did not feel sick, my sore had healed, and Miss Tina didn't act sad or worried when she checked on me. She led me to a kind of cross-tie area. The lady in white was there, waiting for us.

The lady smiled and rubbed my mouth, then patted my neck. I felt a pinch, as usual. I could feel her hand on my leg, then taking my temperature and doing all the things she had done all the time I lived here. The longer I stood there, the sleepier I felt, until I hung my head and relaxed.

I could feel her tugging at my cast for about forever. As she tugged, my leg felt lighter. At last, I looked behind and saw the cast was gone. I would have been happy about this if I wasn't so sleepy. Then I felt something soft wrap around my leg. It wasn't a cast this time, just a soft wrap, kind of like what they use on my front legs, only thicker.

She and Miss Tina talked all the time. I heard something about changing the wrap daily and another month in the stall before hand-walking. I understood some, but not all.

I had never been hand-walked before, and wasn't really sure what that meant. And although I knew what humans called a month, I'd never tried to count it. I don't know if any horse has.

It turns out a month is a little more than forever. I was still spending every day in my stall, although I could move a lot easier without that heavy thing on my foot.

The only time I saw outside of the stall door was when the ranch man came to clean it. It made me so happy to see him. He picked up the poop and pee while I stuck my head past the wheeled bucket and looked outside. The air smelled better out here, and the wind felt cooler. I wished he would come more than once a day.

"Mom," I said, "do you think if I peed and pooped more the ranch man would come more?"

"No. First they would complain about how dirty your stall is. Then they would tell Tina or Niki, who would get worried there was something wrong with you. If you kept it up, the doctor would come and examine you, and you might even end up back in the hospital."

I gave up on that plan. I didn't want to go back into the hospital.

"I don't know why you are complaining," Lulu said. Lulu was the black mare in the end stall. "I'd rather not leave my stall at all, if it meant I would not be used as a lesson horse for incompetents."

Sometimes Lulu said things I didn't understand. "What's incomp-incompetts?"

"Riders who have no business on a horse. They have no balance, they kick me when I clearly hear Niki tell them to squeeze, they yank my face right and left, and don't even give me the chance to stop when they say 'Ho'. They just pull my head back." She blew air from her nose. "It's not their fault. They need to learn from someone. Wendy likes to teach them. I do not."

I had to admit, it sounded like Wendy's job, and Wendy's job sounded hard. "That must be hard for you. But aren't you at least happy to be in the sunshine and stretch your legs?"

She snorted at me. "I am a show horse. I've been to lots of shows and won lots of ribbons. To be relegated to teaching beginners is an insult. If they're not going to show me, I wish they'd either find someone who wants to, or just, just, put me down."

"Oh, Lulu, no. You are not an old horse, and you are healthy."

"But I am not happy. I am not being used for what I can do."

I wondered if she had a lot of owners and if any of them treated her with as much kindness as MomToo treated me. "Maybe you need someone to love you."

"I've had that," she replied. "Yes, it was wonderful to have a human pay so much attention to me. Yes, I miss it, a little. But I miss being useful more. I know what I am. I am a show horse. Asking me to do anything else makes me unhappy. And when I'm unhappy, I don't think I make the beginners happy, and I know I don't make Niki happy."

Just then, Hilde walked into my stall and put my halter on. He patted my neck, then I felt a little pinch. I thought maybe I was going back to the hospital, but he took my halter off and left. I wasn't sure what to think, but the sting didn't make me feel sleepy, so I figured I wasn't going anywhere. As a matter of fact, the pinch made me feel pretty happy.

Later, Auntie Niki came to my stall and put my halter on. This time, she led me out. There was a stud chain on my stall door. It was cold and hard, but fun to chew on if I could get it in my mouth They had used it on me before, putting it over my nose when they longed me. Auntie Niki started using it the day I tried to run away with the long line and almost pulled her off her feet.

This time, she put the stud chain around my halter and put it in my mouth. I was happy to be able to chew on it, but instead, she put it in between my upper lip and my teeth, so that if I didn't stand very still, it rubbed on my gums. I didn't like that and tried to shake it loose, but she tugged down a little and it hurt, so I stopped. When I stopped moving, it stopped hurting.

"Sorry, Snoopy," she said. "But I need you to walk today and I know you've been cooped up for a long time. You cannot run and jump on that leg yet."

We both walked together out of the barn, going slow. I was careful to stay with her so the chain would not hurt. She also seemed careful to stay with me, so she didn't have to tug.

My barn had one exit that went downhill to the arena, and one exit that went flat, to the parking lot. We went out the flat exit.

Together, we walked around the corner, around the hot walker. MomToo had her little black toy out, making clicking noises.

"Doctor Fischer says to walk him for 15 minutes a day, but I think his first day we should just try a few times around the walker," Auntie Niki said.

"Probably best, even if he has been Aced," MomToo replied.

I didn't know what 'Aced' meant, but Auntie Niki shook her head. "I don't know if we didn't give him enough or didn't wait long enough, but I don't think the Ace worked. He's still perky."

I wondered how she knew I felt perky, when I was trying so hard to walk with her. We walked around the hot walker one way, then the other. How wonderful it felt, to be outside, walking around on the ranch! Soon, I would be in the wood pen. I just knew it.

And then, we walked back to my stall. Auntie Niki took off my halter and the chain and patted me. "You were a good boy today. Tomorrow we'll walk a little longer."

When she left, I stuck my face against the bars. "Does anyone know what 'Ace' is?"

"I do," Jet said. He hardly ever spoke to me, except to warn me away from all the mares. "They give you a shot and you feel sleepy. Then they say, 'Well, he should be good now. We Aced him'."

I thought about this. "That doesn't sound like what happened. Hilde came in and pinched my neck. Sometimes that makes me sleepy, but this time it made me feel good, like I wanted to run."

"That pinch is called a shot," Mom told me. "And it sounds like Ace doesn't make you sleepy. I wonder when Hilde and Niki will figure that out."

I didn't care whether I felt good or sleepy, as long as they kept getting me out of my stall.

Auntie Niki takes me on my first walk.

CHAPTER THIRTY-EIGHT

Now we started walking every day. It didn't take long for Auntie Niki to decide that Ace didn't make me sleepy. Hilde stopped coming in to pinch my neck, but he did start walking with me. Auntie Niki would hold me on one side, with the chain on my mouth, and Hilde would walk on the other side, with a lead rope.

It was hard to just walk. I was happy to be out of my stall, I wanted to run around and jump and play. After a bit, the chain on my mouth didn't bother me. I shook my head to loosen it as I jumped forward. I could feel Auntie Niki and Hilde working to keep me from doing this, but it seemed like I had a ball of energy in my gut that needed to come out. Also, I wanted to show them that I was still a useful horse, and that this leg pain was a pain that would heal and not a forever pain.

But the pain was still there, and as much as I tried to tell them I was okay, I wondered if it was true. Each day they walked me, I put my weight on my foot and looked normal, even if it did hurt.

Monte came one day and took me out of my stall. He had taken my shoes off while I was in the hospital, but my hooves were growing and needed to be trimmed. I tried to be a good quiet horse, but he saw how excited I was to leave my stall, so he pinched my neck.

By the time he started to work on my hooves, I felt sleepy and didn't want to move around at all. He trimmed them all and made them all round, then led me back. As he did, I heard Miss Tina tell him, "Whatever you just gave him, we need some of that."

After that, when Hilde pinched my neck, it made me feel quiet and sleepy, and Auntie Niki walked me around by herself. We walked for many, many days, almost as many forever days as when I stood in my stall.

Hilde didn't always pinch my neck and make me sleepy. I heard Auntie Niki say they didn't want to use the medicine on me all the time. I don't know why. Then she would go back and use the chain. After being stuck inside for such a long time, I didn't think I could get tired of being outside, but I was having a harder and harder time staying quiet and just walking.

No one was patting me or calling me a good boy much anymore. MomToo would still stop by with carrots, or sometimes an apple, but it seemed like I had become a job for my humans. Maybe a harder job than the kind Wendy does.

Soon they took the wrap off my leg and left it off. I looked at it. There was a line above my hoof that wasn't there before. I remembered what Valentino said about the surgery, and figured this was where they cut my leg. The hair had mostly grown back. My foot was hurting less, too. Even if no one said I was a good boy, this made me happy. If I couldn't be good, maybe soon I would go back to being useful.

One day, Miss Tina put me on the long rope. I was excited. This meant I was going to longe again, and maybe even be ridden. We went to the wood pen. It had been a long time since I had been in here, not since my leg hurt the first time.

It felt so good, I wanted to show her I was all better, so I tried to jump and buck and run, but she kept stopping me and telling me, "Here." That's what they said when they wanted me to slow down. But I couldn't slow down. I was so happy, I wanted to show it. Miss Tina finally stopped me and led me out of the wood pen.

I thought we were going back to my stall, but she took me to the big arena. I was still on the long rope, but I didn't know what I would do now. I had never been in the arena without a saddle and rider.

Miss Tina let out the line and I was going to run, but there was a pole in my way, so I trotted instead. There was another pole, so I trotted over that. I kept going in a circle, trotting over poles. I couldn't run because there was always another pole to pick my feet up over.

This was a lot of fun, even though it was hard to pick up my broken foot. I couldn't bend it the way I used to, and had to pick up my whole leg with my hip and swing it across. *Trot, trot, trot, swing.* After a bit, Miss Tina asked me to lope the poles. This was easy to the right, but hard to the left. My left hip had to lift my leg high to get it across. *Lope, lope, lope, lift.* We did this forever, until I was sweaty and tired. It felt good.

Afterward, I got a shower and stood on the hot walker to dry, like I used to do. Even better, when Hilde led me back, he took me to my old stall in the barn with Bubba. I was so happy to go back to work. Maybe tomorrow I would be ridden.

CHAPTER THIRTY-NINE

The next morning, the ranch men gave me my breakfast. I ate it for a bit, then I stopped. My stomach felt funny. My leg was kind of sore, too. I laid down and rested. Maybe a nap would make me feel better.

MomToo came to see me. She asked me to get up, but I didn't. My stomach was too sore, and my leg didn't feel good. I didn't want her to know my leg didn't feel good. She looked in a few more times, then I heard her talking to Miss Tina, who looked at me, too. Miss Tina made me get up, and walked me around. I didn't limp, but my stomach hurt.

"He may be starting to colic," Miss Tina said. "Let me call Brigid."

I didn't think I was starting to do anything, except not hurt. I don't know why she thought it was my fault.

Doctor Brigid came to visit me. Usually she has cookies, but not this time.

"Need to get your tummy feeling better first," she told me.

Then she stuck a tube up my nose and down my throat. It is not a nice thing to do to a horse, but then she put the end of the tube in a bucket of water and something, and pumped it into my stomach. She sucked on the end and held it down, so that stuff in my stomach ran out onto the ground. It was icky, but I let her do it without fussing too much.

This was my Doctor Brigid, after all. If she didn't bring cookies today, she would bring them sometime.

At last, she pulled the tube out and told Miss Tina and Auntie Niki a bunch of things I didn't understand. What I did understand was that I was not to get any dinner tonight, and no breakfast tomorrow, and they were to check on my poop, and give me a very little bit of food in the evening, only if my poop looked normal.

Humans are very interested in horse poop. It must be special.

My stomach felt much better, and I gave them a really nice poop to talk about. That night, I dreamed of being in a show. I was loping over poles, into a box. The box had teeth that grabbed my leg and bit me. I woke up and spent the rest of the night staring at the wall, hoping my leg was getting better and not worse.

The next day, I stayed in my stall again. This was okay, since my foot kind of hurt from the day before, and I wanted it to feel better before Miss Tina took me over any more poles. All of the ranch men and Auntie Niki and Miss Tina stopped by to see if I was pooping. They were so happy to see I was, they gave me dinner. It wasn't a lot of dinner, but I ate it up.

After that, Miss Tina longed me over poles again. It was fun, even though my foot hurt. I tried not to show it, but one day I couldn't lift my leg over the pole any more. It was just too hard and my foot hurt too much.

"He's limping again," Miss Tina told MomToo. "Brigid thinks longeing him over poles might work the leg too much. We should maybe back off for a while."

The next day, they put me on the hot walker. I felt the pull of the chain and started walking. My leg didn't hurt, so it was okay. I was very sad, thinking they didn't even want to walk with me anymore. I was worse than just a job for them.

CHAPTER FORTY

Every day, I walked on the hot walker. I tried to be good, but it was hard, and sometimes I would jump and buck and Auntie Niki would stop me and tell me to settle down. I didn't want to settle down. It felt good to be outside and it was easy to get excited when there were other horses on the hot walker, too.

One day, I got really jumpy, so Miss Tina said, "I think he needs a little time on the Patience Tree."

The Patience Tree is a tree on the quiet side of the wood pen. It has a rope that is stretchy and if you are a horse who doesn't want to stand still, they will tie you to the stretchy rope and let you stand there until you stop moving around and relax. I had only been tied to the Patience Tree one time, enough to remember that I could still swing my body around so I didn't have to stand very still. It wasn't like the cross-ties.

That day, I couldn't hold still. I chewed on the tree for a while, then I licked the outside of the wood pen. After forever, I started to get itchy. My fly spray had worn off, so I rubbed my neck against anything that scratched my itch.

Suddenly I felt a pain in my neck and I pulled back. Auntie Niki came over to see what happened, then unhooked me and led me to the cross-ties.

She called to Miss Tina. "Looks like he cut himself open pretty bad."

"On what?" Miss Tina sounded annoyed.

"There's a little bolt on the pen over by the tree. You can always trust Snoopy to find the one sharp object to slice his neck open."

After a bit, one of the doctors came in and looked at my neck. She cleaned the cut and put my skin together and used a little stick to make everything stay in place. Miss Tina said they were stitches. Then the vet gave Miss Tina some medicine to feed me, and left.

MomToo saw me the next day. "Snoopy." She sounded disappointed. "Can you please stop costing me extra money now? I swear you know whenever my bank account has a few dollars in it."

I don't know about money or banks. I just know if I hadn't broken my leg, I wouldn't be tied to the Patience Tree, and if I hadn't been tied to the Patience Tree, I wouldn't have found that bolt.

CHAPTER FORTY-ONE

The next day, it was back to the hot walker without a stop at the Patience Tree. My foot wasn't as sore, but my brain was tired. I had seen everything around the hot walker, too many times. First there was Mom's barn, then the barn with the outside stalls, then the big holes where they keep the new and used bedding. After that were some trees I wasn't allowed to eat, the wood pen, and some more trees. The cross-ties were next, then my barn, the lower arena, and back to Mom's barn.

Turning around and going the other way did not make it interesting. It just gave me a glimpse of the cars in the parking lot.

One day, someone forgot about me getting loose from the hot walker, and they hooked me up by my halter like a normal horse. I walked around a few times, then tested the clip holding me. It came off really easy.

I was a free horse.

The first thing I did was run. I ran to the top of the hill where Bonnie and Snowy were, and said hello. The ranch men were up there, too. They tried to corner me into a stall, but I wasn't done yet. I turned and raced down the hill, thinking I could probably run around in the arenas for a while if nobody caught me. Then I saw something that surprised me.

At the bottom of the hill, Auntie Niki stood, with a lead rope in her hands and an unhappy look on her face.

I tried to stop my legs from moving but my body was going so fast and my feet were on slippery leaves and loose dirt. As I pulled up, my back feet slid underneath me, so much that I kind of sat down as I stopped.

MomToo was at the bottom of the hill, too. She had seen what I did and was yelling. "Not the back leg!"

Auntie Niki walked up toward me, so I turned and ran up the hill again. This time, the ranch guys stopped me and Auntie Niki got the lead rope on my halter and led me back to my stall.

My leg might hurt later, but it sure felt good to run a little.

The next day, I was back on the hot walker and the next and the next, until I thought all I would do for the rest of my life was walk in circles. MomToo was riding Mom. No one was riding me. I wasn't useful anymore, and it was harder and harder to be good.

When I was in the other barn, I would see MomToo go to Mom's stall and talk about different things. She usually said something about how Mom shouldn't worry, that I'd be okay, but then she talked about her human family and what else she was doing.

One day in the cross-ties, I asked Mom about it. "Why does MomToo talk about her family so much with you?"

"She likes to talk and I like to listen."

"Do you understand what she says?"

"Most of the time. I have a bigger vocabulary than you, Snoopy, and I've got a very old spirit, so I remember a lot of what I have seen and heard."

"What's a vocabulary?"

"The words I know. So when Gayle tells me about her husband and her son, I know that she is married to a man and they had a baby, much like you are my son. Even when I don't understand the exact words, I understand her feelings. For example, today she talked about going on a vacation. I'm not certain what a vacation is, but I could feel that she was trying to tell me she would be away for many days and nights. She doesn't understand that I don't care about time the way she does, but I appreciate that she tells me I will be taken care of while she is away."

"Did she ever ride you in shows?"

"Yes, for a little while. I do not like shows. They are noisy, and nothing is the same. I am always worried about things going wrong."

"You sound like Wendy," I told her.

"Wendy and I do not like shows. Gayle tried to make me like them, but she also gets worried about things, which makes me worry more."

"Did she tell you she was worried?"

"No, no, it was in the way she rode. When we are at home, she is quiet and calm in the arena. She can even ride me over poles, which I do not like to do, and I go over them quietly. But in the show arena, she was nervous and I felt it from her hands, through her balance, down to her feet. This made me nervous as well. When we tried to do poles and everyone was watching us and she was tense, well, we didn't do well."

"I love shows, Mom." I remembered the first one, when I got my mane banded and wore a shiny saddle. "They're so much fun, full of humans and other horses. There's so much to see, and the poles are so pretty. I like to show everyone what I can do."

"I'm so glad you like it," Mom said. "One thing I worried about most was that Gayle would sell me when she realized I was not a show horse. But instead, she let me have a baby, and it's good that you can be her show horse."

Although I was happy to hear this, it bothered me, too. "So if I was not her show horse, she would sell me?"

"I don't know. She likes to go to horse shows, and I do not believe she can keep two horses who do not show. She would either sell you or me. Although I am now the more sellable horse, I know how much she loves me and would rather not part with me. She could always breed me again and hope for another baby who liked to show."

"But when I get better, I will show again, right?"

Mom didn't answer me at first. "Your leg was hurt badly. In addition, the humans cut your leg open and put metal inside. It may take a long time to heal. It may not heal enough for you to show again."

I think she felt how sad she was making me, so she added, "But you should certainly believe that your leg will heal and you will return to the show arena."

Between thinking about possibly not showing again, and MomToo possibly selling me, it was a very sad day inside my head. I wondered how Valentino was doing, and I remembered Kid Galahad and his awful end.

"Mom," I nickered. "Do all horses go to the Clover Fields?"

"I do not know it for a fact, but I believe it is so."

"Do you think, if MomToo sold me, I would still be loved?"

"Snoopy, you are loved now. If it comes to that and you cannot be shown, or cannot stay here, I am certain Gayle will only let you go to a better home than she can give you." She added, "And Snoopy, I know Gayle. She is a stubborn human. When she first bought me, she was actually afraid when she rode me, and thought constantly about stopping and getting off during our lessons together. But she never gave up. She won't give up on you, either."

MomToo led Mom down to the arena, so we couldn't talk anymore, but I felt a little happier after talking to her.

CHAPTER FORTY-TWO

The days got colder and the sun did not shine as long, and still I was walked. One day, Miss Tina got me out of my stall and led me down to the big arena. I was excited. Maybe I would be longed over poles again.

Instead, we went to the little cart and she sat on the back. Auntie Niki was in the front.

"Go ahead," Miss Tina said.

Auntie Niki did something to the wheel in her hands and the cart started to roll. As it moved, Miss Tina held my lead rope and I walked behind. The cart went faster, so I walked faster, until I was trotting. We went all around the big arena this way, Auntie Niki moving the wheel, Miss Tina holding my rope, and me trotting.

It wasn't quite as much fun as loping the poles, but it was pretty fun.

After a bit, they stopped. Miss Tina handed me to MomToo and she brushed me all over, then put me back in my stall.

"Maybe this will work, Snoopy," MomToo said as she put my blanket on. "You can trot in a straight line longer behind the golf cart. It's better for your leg."

I stuck my nose out, trying to grab the blanket from her. She spanked me, but she didn't act mad at me.

When I saw Mom the next day, she said, "You see? She's not ready to give up. That means you can't, either."

My foot hurt the next day, but they let me rest, so I didn't have to hide it from anyone. The day after that, I chased the little cart again, then rested a day, then chased the cart. It was fun, but after a bit, my foot still hurt from the days before. I tried to keep Miss Tina from noticing.

I couldn't hide it forever, and suddenly I was back on the hot walker.

I began to accept that this was my life. I would stand in my stall, then walk on the walker, then stand in my stall. There would be no more running, no more riding, no more poles. Perhaps I would go to another owner who didn't mind that I just walked.

MomToo would need a better horse.

My dreams that used to be about running and bucking stopped. Instead, I dreamed about standing in the arena and wanting to run, but my feet were stuck in the ground. In one dream, Miss Tina tried to sell me, and I couldn't get my feet to move at all. I woke up when she said, "I guess it's time for the teal truck."

MomToo still brushed and massaged me. She talked to me about getting better, and I tried to be a happy horse for her. My heart just didn't feel happy.

I'm chasing the cart.

CHAPTER FORTY-THREE

It was still a little cold, but the sun was staying longer, when Miss Tina came into my stall and pinched my neck. I felt a little sleepy, and she put on my halter and led me out of my stall toward the parking lot. I thought maybe I would go in the moving box, but instead, we walked right out of the gate onto the street. Auntie Niki and MomToo went with us.

It was a nice walk in the sun. I got to see lots of stuff, like a field of grass and strange barns and horses. We walked past a barn I knew. It was where the horses were jumping the first time I was in the hospital.

That's where we were going. I didn't know why I would be here again. I didn't feel bad. They put me in the pen that was outside my window the last time I stayed here. I thought about Kid Galahad and shuddered. That was an awful time.

Everyone went inside for a bit, then the lady in white came out and led me out of the pen. MomToo and Auntie Niki were there.

"I haven't seen Snoopy in a long time," the lady said. "Why are we seeing him today?"

"It's been ten months and he's still not trotting," MomToo told her.

I didn't understand what ten months meant, but I wanted to tell them MomToo was wrong. I *was* trotting, sort of.

Auntie Niki led me out of the pen.

"He looks like he's walking fine," the lady said.

"Oh he walks just fine," MomToo told her. "But his trot is... no good."

That was true.

Then Miss Tina came over with a bunch of men in white. They felt the heels of my back legs and talked about it, but I couldn't understand their words. Then one of the men told Auntie Niki to make me trot.

I was awake by now and felt pretty good about showing off, so I didn't really want to trot straight. I wanted to jump a little. I trotted, but I kept getting excited and wiggling.

"You're right," the man said. "He's not trotting well."

The lady in white took my lead rope and led me to the big empty stall with the silver box in it. Once again, they made me hold my foot quiet, then I heard clicking noises. After that, they led me to a place that looked like our cross-ties at home, except there were no chains for me to chew.

A strange man held my lead rope while the lady in white did something to my broken leg. The man's shirt was very soft. I reached out and grabbed it. Auntie Niki would have spanked me, but he just pushed my mouth away. This was going to be a fun game.

I felt something cold on my leg, so I lifted it. The lady made me put my foot down, but I felt the cold again, so I picked it up again. This was a fun game, too. Between grabbing the man and playing with the lady, I was having a pretty good time.

I had just found the tree next to the man and was reaching for some leaves when I felt a pinch on my neck. Soon, I was sleepy and the games were over.

The man in white did all the talking, but I was sleepy and didn't want to listen. Auntie Niki and Miss Tina weren't there anymore, just MomToo. Doctor Brigid came and gave me a cookie, which was good.

The man put me back in the pen, and after forever, Auntie Niki and MomToo came and walked me home. The sleepy pinch was gone again, and I wanted to skip and run and eat grass on the way home, but Auntie Niki said no. As we walked, MomToo explained what the man said.

"Doctor Fischer says there's a difference between his right and left pasterns. The angle of the left one is lower. He thinks it's a stretched suspensory ligament. Basically tendonitis. He said he thought the ligament looked swollen on the ultrasound. He recommends sixty days of hand-walking, then another ultrasound."

All I really understood was hand-walking.

Auntie Niki mostly nodded while she kept tugging on my lead rope to keep me from jumping. "So, how much hand-walking?"

"Thirty to forty-five minutes a day."

By the time we got back to my stall, I could feel both happy and sad in MomToo. "Ah, Snoopy," she told me. "It's a lot longer road than I imagined. Doctor Fischer said you'd be back to work in six months. It's been ten."

I still didn't know how to count months, but I could tell by the way she said it, she meant forever.

I'm waiting to see the doctor.

CHAPTER FORTY-FOUR

The next day, I was back to the hot walker. I was sad. I didn't even feel like talking to the other horses in the barn any more. More than anything, I wished I understood the words MomToo said about my leg and I wished I could hear her happiness, instead of her worry.

The day Doctor Pollard came, I was almost crazy with sadness. Auntie Niki led me out to him and MomToo. I felt a sharp pinch in my heel, then another and another. Then we walked to the upper arena and stood around.

Doctor Pollard talks so low and nice, that even if I don't understand him, I like to listen to him. He told Auntie Niki something about giving the blocker time to work. I wasn't sure what that meant, but I understood the next thing he said.

"Go ahead and trot him."

I was very excited to be in the upper arena and trotting, so I trotted as hard as I could. It felt funny, because I couldn't feel my broken foot at all. I lifted it super high to keep it from dragging in the dirt, and I couldn't tell when it hit the ground. I guess it was hard for Auntie Niki to keep up with me. She kept tugging me to slow down, but I would just step sideways.

It was fun, but I heard Doctor Pollard say, "Okay, Niki, bring him back."

We walked back over to the doctor, who had a little stick in his hand. "I didn't see any difference when we blocked his hoof, so I'm going to move up to the fetlock."

I felt more pinching, higher up in my leg. We stood around, then Auntie Niki trotted me again. Or tried to. I couldn't feel much of my leg at all, so I could trot really fast. Auntie Niki kept tugging at me and stopping, and trying again. I'm afraid we were both a little sideways by the end.

"I wouldn't call him one hundred percent better," Doctor Pollard said. "But he's a good eighty percent with the fetlock block. I'm going to write up what I did and what the results were, so you can talk to the folks at UC Davis about what we've done. I'll also get you his X-rays, so all you'd need is his ultrasound."

I understood very few of his words, but MomToo looked happy. If she had hope, I needed to have it, too.

Instead of going back to my stall in the barn, Auntie Niki led me to an open stall in front of the jumping horses. I could look down into the wood pen, and see both the upper arena and part of the lower arena. There were no neighbors in the stalls next to mine, but at the end, there was a chestnut paint mare. She was smaller than Bonnie.

"Hello," I said. "My name's Snoopy. What's yours?"

"Rose." I watched her twirl around in her stall, then lay her ears back and shake her head at me. "I saw what they did to you out in the arena. That Niki is a horrible person."

I wasn't sure what horrible meant, but from her voice it sounded bad. "Auntie Niki? She's very nice to me."

"Nice? You call that nice, the way she dragged you around the arena with that awful chain on your nose? I'm surprised it didn't leave marks. I'll bet you have bruises."

"Oh, the chain didn't hurt. I was feeling really good and wanted to trot fast. She can't trot that fast."

"Don't defend her. She's always making me do things I don't want to do."

I was surprised that my Auntie Niki would do this. "That's too bad. I always have fun when I'm with her."

"Even when she makes you go in that pen and run on a line?"

"That's fun, though. I haven't been able to run on a line in forever. It would make me very happy to do that again."

"Oh, yes, I heard about you. You're the broken horse."

The way she said this made me feel bad. "I'm not broken. I just have a broken leg. But I'm getting better."

She snorted. "According to who? And better than what?"

"The doctor thinks I'm getting better. He said today I was eighty cent." I hadn't understood these words, but I thought she needed me to explain. "If I keep getting better, I can be longed on the line again, and even ridden again, and maybe go to shows again."

"Are you some kind of weirdo? You broke your leg. You should be out in some pasture somewhere, hanging out and living large."

"But Miss Tina won't let us in the pasture anymore, and I don't know how to live any other way than as a big horse. As for hanging out, only when I'm kind of relaxed—"

"No, no, no." She twirled around again. "I mean, somewhere else, in a proper pasture with a herd of horses. You should be spending your days eating grass and scratching other horses' withers and rolling in the dirt. Not wearing heavy shoes and taking orders from humans. They're either mean or they're weak."

I didn't understand this mare at all. "But I love my humans. They scratch me and pet me and tell me I'm a good boy. When they ride me at shows and I feel everyone watching me, it's fun. When I win, I feel so much happiness all around me, from my humans and even from my friend, Bubba."

"Chumps. You are all chumps. Horses were meant to be free and live without humans. We shouldn't be slaves to some two-legged beast's whims. They're smaller than us, anyway. What right do they have to tell us what to do?"

"They're our humans and they love us," was all I could say.

Although this was our first time talking, each time after, we talked about the same thing again, and again, and again. She didn't like Auntie Niki and didn't like being ridden and thought it was not natural, from wearing bits to shoes. Even if I just said good morning, Rose always talked about the same thing.

Talking to Rose was the closest I ever came to feeling bored.

CHAPTER FORTY-FIVE

Lots of days passed. I walked on the hot walker. I watched Rose fight with Auntie Niki and ignore her owner. Each time I saw her on the long rope, I wished it was me, and wanted even more to be ridden again.

Then one day, I woke up feeling like I would never be ridden again. I didn't know why. It had just been so long since I carried anyone on my back, and so long since I was able to run around. I guess I gave up. Suddenly I had no answer for Rose about what a horse should and shouldn't do. I had never thought about whether Auntie Niki or MomToo had the right to tell me what to do.

I wasn't even sure if I knew what a right was. When I was little, my humans asked me to do things. When I did them, they scratched and patted me and I was happy. Later, when I was older and started doing things they didn't want me to do, they spanked me. It didn't hurt as bad as Uncle Snowy's teeth or hooves. But it made me want to do the right thing instead of the wrong thing. Did I have a *right* to more than that?

The rest of the day, I thought about what Rose had been saying all the time. Should I go be in a pasture with other horses now, instead of trying to go back to being a show horse? It would be easier. I could run and jump with no human to stop me. If my leg hurt, I could stand still, or walk a little. I wouldn't have to work anymore.

Was the work really that fun? Or did I just like my humans to be happy? Did it make me happy?

It was a hard night's sleep. I dreamed of a green pasture. Lots of horses were there, horses I didn't know. I was eating grass. It was good. I was happy. Then I saw Miss Tina's truck drive by, with the big moving box chasing it. Bubba was inside, calling to me.

"Snoopy! Snoopy, why aren't you going to the show with me?"

I galloped toward the truck, but it went too fast and I couldn't catch it. I stopped and went back to my herd. That's when I saw two faces I recognized. Holly and Uno were in the pasture with me. I looked down and saw apples on the ground.

"Welcome, Snoopy," Holly said. "You're in the Clover Fields now."

I woke up. It was still dark, but I rose and walked around my stall a few times, shaking my head to shake the dream out. That's when I heard something in the paddock above me. It was Uncle Snowy. I couldn't see him, because the jumper barn was in my way, but he didn't sound well.

"Uncle Snowy. Are you all right?"

I heard him moan a little. "My stomach hurts."

"Should we call for Miss Tina, or the ranch men?" I remembered my stomach hurting, and Doctor Brigid making it feel better.

"Miss Tina is not home." He was quiet for a little bit. "It's not just my stomach, Snoopy. I am feeling so old, so tired. I am an old, old pony tonight."

"Oh, no, Uncle Snowy. You are still young. Remember when you used to chase me up and down our paddock?"

"Snoopy, that was a long time ago. It's all right. I am ready to move on. I am not being ridden anymore, so my days are all the same. I haven't had a young horse to boss around since you were little. Frankly, it's boring. If I am not being useful, I might as well join Holly and Uno and my other friends in the Clover Fields. I am looking forward to having young bones again. Maybe I'll even jump."

I stayed awake the rest of the night, listening for any sign that he was hurting too bad. Sometimes I heard him moan a little, and a few times, I heard him whisper, "Just a little bit longer." It took forever for the sun to shine, and even longer for Auntie Niki to walk up the hill.

She led Uncle Snowy down to the barn. He had grown a lot of hair and was very shaggy. I could see the pain in his eyes as he walked by.

"Your temperature is up, old man," Auntie Niki said. "And you're breathing really hard."

They walked to the wood pen and she turned him loose. He walked to the center and stood, his head hanging down.

"Hang on," she told him. "I'm calling Dr. Pollard."

"Uncle Snowy," I called out. "Are you all right?"

He shook his mane. "Don't worry, Snoopy. Niki says the doctor's on his way. The teal truck won't be far behind him, and I'll be rolling in clover soon."

"Please don't leave. I'll miss you too much."

"I'll miss you, too, but it's time for me to go. This is forever pain." He stopped for a moment and lifted his head to look at me. I could see the pain in his eyes. "You never know. I'm such a good teacher, I may be back soon. In the meantime, be a good horse and stop biting. And get back in that show arena. You know it's where you want to be."

With his last word, he lowered his head and fell to his knees, then rolled to his side. Auntie Niki ran to the pen and opened the door. I watched her look at him. He was looking back at her. She was crying a little.

"Are you done, old man?"

"Yes," he told her, although I don't know if she could hear.

I saw Doctor Pollard's truck roll in. He got out and walked to the wood pen, then took out all his silver toys and put them on Uncle Snowy. The whole time, he talked to Auntie Niki. I saw him take a stick out of his bag and pinch Uncle Snowy's neck. Uncle Snowy breathed once, twice, then was silent. He was on his way to the Clover Fields.

Sometimes I wished I was human so I could cry. I had seen MomToo do it. It felt like her sadness was water that filled her inside and spilled out of her eyes. My sadness was not water. It was heavy, like the poles I tried to pick up, and it filled my body so that I could not move.

Rose was telling me something but I wasn't listening. I was thinking about my friend.

Uncle Snowy taught me so much when I was little. He told me not to kick or bite other horses, or to throw goats, and that humans would be nice to me if I was a good horse. Now as he was leaving me, he took the time to give me one more lesson.

I was to go back to being a show horse.

CHAPTER FORTY-SIX

The next day, MomToo came to see me. First, she brought a curry and brush, and groomed and massaged me all over. That felt good. Then Miz Cee came into my stall. They put a soft wrap around my broken leg. I tried to ask Miz Cee how Bubba was, but she didn't speak horse any better than MomToo.

After a bit, a strange man walked in, and MomToo put my halter on. The man's name was Chuck.

"Be careful," MomToo told him. "He's very mouthy, and he gets pretty excited when you take him out of his stall. He might want to dance to the trailer."

I remembered Uncle Snowy's words, to be a good horse, so I put my head down and walked with Chuck. I tried not to look at him, so I wouldn't want to feel his shirt with my mouth. We walked past the wood pen, to the parking lot, and the street. Chuck had the biggest moving box I had ever seen.

He walked me up the slanted piece and put me in cross-ties. There were no other horses in the box, and I had lots of room to wiggle back and forth. I had a big bag of hay in front of me, too. Everything in Chuck's was big.

The door closed, but there was still light from the windows. I couldn't see the trees go sideways, but the floor moved up and down and I was happy to eat. We moved for a long time. I knew I wasn't going to a show, and it was too long to be going to the hospital, so I didn't know where Chuck was taking me.

Suddenly, I got scared that I was going to a new home. I didn't get to say goodbye to anyone, especially Mom. But MomToo hadn't been very sad. She would be sad if I went to a new home, wouldn't she?

After forever, we stopped. The doors opened and another strange man led me out to a parking lot.

I heard a familiar voice "Be careful with him. He's really mouthy."

It was MomToo. I was surprised and happy to see her there. She was talking to a lady in white. There were familiar smells coming from the barns.

This was another hospital.

I didn't know what they were going to do, so I walked quietly with the man, who took off my soft wrap and put me in a stall. MomToo met up with two men in white coats. They touched their hands together, like I've seen humans do, then went away for a while. I learned that one of the men was Doctor Martinelli, and the other one was Doctor Rantanen, and the lady in white was Doctor Walker. They were hard names to remember. Why couldn't humans have normal names, like Bubba or Holly?

I had hay to eat in this stall, so I was happy.

After a bit, the strange man led me out of the stall and down to an open area of dirt. MomToo and the two men in white were there. The strange man made me trot. I trotted very straight and stayed with him the whole time. And I did not grab his shirt.

"Watch out for him," Doctor Martinelli said to the man. "He's really mouthy."

MomToo laughed. "Trust me, this is not like him. Talk to the people at Chino Valley."

They didn't know I was trying to be good. It was the least I could do for Uncle Snowy.

"Wow, he's really lame," Dr. Martinelli said.

I saw MomToo nod. They brought me to a place that reminded me of the other hospital. It was hard, like cross-ties, but the strange man held my lead rope.

Doctor Walker pinched my neck and I felt sleepy. Then I felt something cold on the back of my broken leg. It moved up and down and sideways, sometimes stopping. Looking behind me, I saw Doctor Rantanen sitting at my foot and running a box around on it. He was looking at another box, pointing and talking to MomToo.

Doctor Martinelli was talking, too. They were talking about bone scans and stem cells and stuff I couldn't understand.

After forever, Doctor Rantanen turned to MomToo and pointed to the box he had been watching. He said, "I know he trots like he's lame, but if this was a million-dollar racehorse and had a race tomorrow, I couldn't give you a doctor's note to get him out of it. His bones have fused properly, and I can't find any ligament damage."

MomToo smiled, and I could feel a bit of happiness, like a little speck of sun in her heart.

Then Doctor Martinelli spoke. "Doctor Rantanen can't find any soft tissue damage, so there's no need to do shock wave or stem cell treatment. Snoopy's X-rays show that the bones are fused properly. So basically, there's nothing wrong with him, except that he's lame.

"I think, although radiologically, he's fused, functionally, he hasn't. He just still hurts from the initial injury and surgery. I won't give you a one-hundred-percent guarantee that he'll end up completely sound, but I think right now it's still too soon to tell.

"In the meantime, I think you should take the kid gloves off and let him be a horse. Turn him out, don't worry if he runs around and kicks up his heels. If he's quiet enough, ride him at the walk. Just don't let him do any reining slides again."

I didn't understand most of it, but I did know what *let him be a horse* meant. And *running and kicking up my heels*? Count me in.

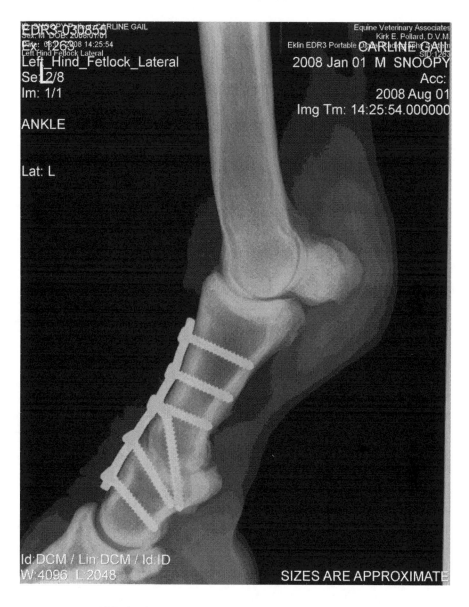

This is the picture MomToo showed the doctors.

CHAPTER FORTY-SEVEN

Once we got home, there were lots of changes. First, I was moved to a bigger stall. It was up on the hill where I could see everything. Bonnie was two stalls away from me, so I wasn't alone. There were sheep now in the pasture. I remembered the fun I had with the goats, but I was pretty sure they wouldn't put me in the pasture and let me throw the sheep around.

Sadly, I was across from where Uncle Snowy and I had spent so much time. I missed him, but promised to be a good horse and get back to the show arena. At least, I was going to try.

Later, Auntie Niki brought me down and put all kinds of protection on my front feet, from bell boots to polo wraps. Then she put the long rope on me, with a stud chain.

At last, I was going to be longed.

Auntie Niki tried to make me trot, but I was just so excited. MomToo stood outside and watched. "Tina wants me to trot him each way for five minutes," Auntie Niki told her. "But I think the best we'll get is if I lope him for three minutes."

Five minutes, three minutes, none of that meant a thing to me. I just tried to keep from jumping for joy, and loped quietly, each direction. Although in my head, I wanted to keep loping, my body got very tired. By the time Auntie Niki stopped me and led me out, I was sweaty and breathing hard.

"He has no stamina," she said. "We'll have to build that back up."

This became my routine, to longe on the line each direction every day. I soon felt good enough to trot most of the way and lope a little. The difference between this time and the times before was that, instead of stopping when my leg hurt, Auntie Niki made me go further.

At first it was hard and I wanted to try to hide my pain, but when I realized they weren't going to stop, I limped when I had to. If MomToo was there, Auntie Niki would talk about what she was doing.

"See how short-strided he is on that leg? We need to push him, gently, to keep moving it out a little further and see if he can get it to even out more with the other leg. He may never be equal. Hell, he's got a fused joint. But he should be able to get his hip unlocked, build up the muscle tone, and move more freely."

I didn't know what she was talking about, but the tone of her voice said she was happy with my broken leg and that not only could I get better, I *was* getting better.

Later, they moved me from the bigger stall, to the even bigger paddock, the one I had shared with Mom and with Uncle Snowy.

"It's on a hill," Miss Tina said. "He will have to use that leg to walk up to get his feed and down to get his water."

It wasn't easy to walk up and down my paddock. First, it made me sad to miss Uncle Snowy. Also, it made my hip and bottom sore to push myself up the hill, then hold myself back going down. But as the days went by, I started to feel stronger.

One morning, Auntie Niki took me into the barn before longeing me. She put a saddle on my back. Maybe today she was going to ride me.

Except she didn't. We longed as usual, trotting, then loping, then trotting. I was very sweaty when I was done.

"Good Snoopy," she said. "Once you are strong enough with a saddle on your back, we'll get on you."

I figured this was just like when I was being taught to wear a saddle. Only this time, it wasn't about learning. It was about being strong enough to do it. I had to admit, the saddle felt heavier than I remembered, and longeing still made me very tired. As long as I knew I would be ridden again, I was happy to keep wearing the saddle and doing as Auntie Niki said.

We did this every day for lots of days. The sun was shining longer and longer, and it was hotter. One warm afternoon, I was brought down for my longe. Auntie Niki put the saddle on and took me to the wood pen. The saddle was feeling much better on my back, and I was able to keep loping longer. After I was pretty sweaty and tired, Auntie Niki led me over to the box in the middle of the pen. That's when I noticed she had a bridle and reins with her. She put them on me, then climbed on my back.

I was finally strong enough to ride. This made me very happy. We walked around the wood pen a few times. My leg was tired, but my heart was full. She got off and patted me. "Well, the leg felt draggy, but you were a good horse."

Our routine changed to include her riding me around the wood pen at the walk. It was the same, every day, but I was happy. I was working to get stronger. If I got stronger, we could go to the big arena. If I got really strong, I could go over the poles again.

My dreams started to be about trail courses and horse shows.

CHAPTER FORTY-EIGHT

Finally, finally, finally the day was here and Auntie Niki was riding me in the big arena. We still just walked, and we didn't go over any poles, but we were where I wanted to be. After our walk, I got a bath, then I was put back in my old, old stall by the arena, where I used to be with Rusty and Wendy. Rusty was gone, but Wendy was there, along with a new mare, Rags. Rags was pretty friendly, except when she warned me to stay away from her food.

"She's the new lesson horse," Wendy said. "They sold Lulu to someone who wanted to show her again, so Rags is taking her place."

"I like being a lesson horse here," Rags told me. "It's so easy, especially with the children, and look at all the food I get."

I missed Lulu, but I was glad that she got to do what she wanted, and that Rags was happy to take over and give lessons.

Auntie Niki and I kept doing mostly the same thing every day, except that every few days we added a little more. After walking the arena, we tried jogging around the arena. Finally, we loped around the arena. We weren't going over poles yet, but we were doing more stuff, so I was happy.

One sunny day, Auntie Niki jogged me over a pole. It was in a straight line, and it was hard to do, but I did it, so she found another straight line and we jogged that pole, too. I learned that if I picked my hip up, it kept my broken leg from hitting the poles. My leg got tired, but it felt good to be back in the big arena and on the trail course.

The best thing was, after forever of Auntie Niki riding me, MomToo started riding me a little. She didn't ride me every time she was at the ranch, but I was happy for any time we spent together.

The days got less sunny and a lot colder, and it started raining more. I was moved into a stall inside, in the same barn as Bubba. I was back to where I left off, as a show horse in the show barn with my friend. I just knew, when the rains went away and the days got sunnier, I'd be back at the horse shows. Maybe MomToo would be riding me in them.

One day, a new lady came to see me. Auntie Niki led me out of my stall, and told her about my broken leg. She called the new lady Doctor Bari. I thought Doctor Bari might be fun. She stood on the box in the barn aisle. I like to try to stand on the box, but no one will let me. I felt two hands on my hips, then I felt pressure. I almost fell to my knees.

"Oh, he's out," said Doctor Bari.

She pressed my back and my hips, then my shoulders. Then she got off the box and wiggled my front legs and bent my head around toward her. I tried to grab her when she did, but Auntie Niki held my halter and wouldn't let me chew on her shirt.

"He was pretty bad, but this is his first adjustment," Doctor Bari said. "Give him the day off, then just a light longe tomorrow. You also might want to give him a couple of bute."

Auntie Niki put me back in my stall, then I watched her get Bubba out. Doctor Bari did the same thing to him, pressing and wiggling and stretching his body.

"Bubba, what is Doctor Bari doing to you?" I asked.

"Miz Cee calls it Ki-Ro-Prack-Tick," he told me. "The doctor presses and wiggles your bones back to where they belong. It can make you a little sore, but it's better to have everything in the right place. Keeps you from getting old too fast."

Doctor Bari was very nice, although she didn't give cookies like Doctor Brigid. Very few doctors give cookies. Not even MomToo gives me a lot of them. Doctor Bari kept coming out and seeing me. She didn't like for me to grab her, but not many people did.

"Snoopy can't help it," she told Auntie Niki. "He's ADHD."

I had never heard of 'ai-dee-aich-dee' but it made Auntie Niki laugh.

"Ah, Snoopy," she said as she put me away and patted my neck. "Why do we love such an annoying horse?"

CHAPTER FORTY-NINE

When the days got sunnier and better and the arenas weren't so muddy, I was ridden a lot more. Finally, MomToo started riding me over poles, too. Her balance wasn't quite as good as Miss Tina or Auntie Niki, but she tried really hard to tell me what she wanted. Miss Tina usually sat in the arena and told her what to do. She made MomToo leave my reins long and wouldn't let her lift her hand too much.

"Let him figure it out," she would say.

Sometimes, I figured out what she wanted, and I figured out how many steps to take in between poles. MomToo was happy then. Sometimes I just couldn't understand. The more we did it wrong, the more I would feel MomToo get tense and unbalanced and the more Miss Tina would talk loud. If our ride ended like that, MomToo was unhappy.

The warmer the days became, the more MomToo rode. Miss Tina was always there, telling her to do things. Sometimes it was a good day and sometimes it wasn't. It was after a bath one warm sunny afternoon that MomToo said something scary as she put me in my stall.

"I don't think I'll ever ride well enough to show you."

For all this forever time, I had been worried about getting healed and going to shows and not making MomToo need a better horse. Maybe what MomToo needed was a horse that already knew exactly what to do and did it. That would be a better horse for her, a better one than me.

One morning, Auntie Niki led me to the moving box. I hadn't been clipped or banded or anything, but Bubba was there, too.

"Are we going to a show?" I asked him.

"Yes. Didn't they get you ready?"

"No. Do you think I'll show anyway?"

"Probably not. How long has it been since you went to a show?"

"I don't know. Since before my leg broke."

"If I had to guess," Bubba said. "I'd say they are just taking you to this show to hang out and make sure you remember what a horse show is like."

"Of course I know what a horse show is like. I've been to horse shows before."

"Snoopy, humans are funny. I think they don't remember very well, so they make us do things we've done before. Either that, or they think we forget."

We rode in the moving box for almost forever, until we stopped. I recognized the barns right away and started to call out to everyone. I was so happy to be there. MomToo was there and led me to my stall, but I was too excited and wanted to be outside. She had to spank me a few times to get me away from the door so she could get out.

"I remember this place, Bubba." I was so happy I screamed this. "What's its name?"

"Burbank," he said. "And calm down."

Once MomToo and Auntie Niki had taken everything out of the moving box and it left, they put the long rope and chain on me, along with some boots, and we went to an arena. It had solid brown walls, although they weren't very tall. Even I could have jumped them. On one end there was a big building. On the other end, there was more dirt, and trucks going by.

MomToo found a corner where I could run. I ran and ran, as fast as I could. It was so exciting to be at a horse show. There were other horses in the arena on lines. Some were running, some were trotting. Outside the arena, there were people walking by, and little carts and bicycles.

I said hello to them all as I flew around in a circle. Every time I slowed down, MomToo would stop me and turn me the other direction. It was like a brand new trip, and I would run just as fast this way. Finally, I got too tired to run. I was breathing hard and was very sweaty. MomToo let me trot a few circles both ways, then stopped me and took me to the showers to get cleaned up.

I went back to my stall a tired, happy horse.

Bubba went out after me. I called out to him as he left. I knew he'd come back, but I was still excited about being here. There were lots of stalls on both sides of our barn aisle, and strange horses were all around me. I introduced myself to everyone who walked past.

"Hi, I'm Snoopy. I haven't been here in forever. Who are you?"

Most of the horses ignored me, and a couple of them told me to shut up. A few of the horses were friendly and said they were glad to meet me. It didn't matter. I was happy to see them all.

When Bubba came back, I thought we could talk, but MomToo got me out of my stall and put a saddle on me. Maybe she was going to ride me. Even if I wasn't going to be in the arena with the judges, this could be good. We could have a good ride together and she could feel better and maybe she could show me next time.

We went out with Auntie Niki to the practice arena. There were lots of horses there. They were all going fast. I watched one of them gallop down the middle of the arena. Everyone had to get out of his way, and I thought he was going to jump the short wall and keep galloping.

Suddenly, he sat his bottom down in the dirt and stopped. The dust flew up behind him, and his front legs walked forward a little bit. Just as suddenly, he spun around and galloped the other direction, making everyone scatter.

I remembered what Johnny and Tucker had told me when I was younger. Turn and burn. These were reiners.

As usual, Auntie Niki got on me first, and rode me around the arena. It felt a little funny to be going so slow, when everyone else was going so fast. As I jogged around, I watched some horses stand still in the middle, then quickly pivot on one back leg, three, four, more times around. They stopped just as quickly, and stood still again.

I was a little nervous about being run into, or run over, but Auntie Niki steered me around everyone without any accidents. After she was happy with my walk, jog, and lope, she rode me out of the arena and back to MomToo.

"Did you want a lesson today?" she asked.

I watched MomToo look at the arena of spinning, running horses. *Please say yes,* I told her. *I'll protect you.* I knew how to avoid the horses now.

"No." She pointed to the arena. "I don't think I want to be in the middle of all that."

We went back to the stalls. Now I was tired and sad.

Bubba was eating. I looked at my stall door and saw my bucket full of food. I was at least glad that Bubba was next to me, so we could talk while we ate.

"Bubba, does your owner always ride you in the horse shows?"

"Of course. Why wouldn't she?"

His answer made me feel a little embarrassed.

"Does Auntie Niki or Miss Tina ride you in the show?"

"Only in the warm up, to help me lift my body properly. And only if it's needed. Why are you asking this?"

"Because MomToo—my owner—has never ridden me in the arena with the judges."

"Well, as I remember, your first shows were futurity shows. Usually the trainers ride those anyway."

"Yes, but I went to shows after that, before my broken leg, and MomToo never rode me. And now that I'm back at the shows, she didn't ride me today. What's wrong with me, Bubba?"

"Probably nothing. Some owners ride a lot at home, but lose their confidence at shows. Even Miz Cee sometimes feels a little tense on my back as we go into the arena, more tense than at home."

"But you win a lot anyway, right?"

"Oh, yes. She works very hard to not be so tense, and I work hard to tune out her nerves. We are a good team."

I thought about what he said. I had gotten to be a good team with Miss Tina. Even Auntie Niki was a good partner, although she was more strict about making my shoulders stand up and my hips push forward. Sometimes I wanted to be lazy, but she never let me. I had to work hard on her team.

With MomToo, it was different. Sometimes I didn't understand what she wanted, especially if she was not balanced on me. Sometimes we had really bad rides together when she felt all tight and wanted to tug and jerk and poke me around the poles.

Bubba said it was confidence. MomToo said I was too confident. If I was too confident and MomToo wasn't confident enough, how were we ever going to become a team?

CHAPTER FIFTY

The next day, Bubba got dressed in his show stuff and went to the big arena. I called after him again. There were a couple of other horses with me, both little mares about my age, Gracie and Taylor. Gracie was chestnut and didn't have much to say, except that her owner would be here soon and she needed to be a good girl for her. She just kept repeating it, "Good girl, good girl, I'm going to be a good mare."

Taylor was black, like me. She was excited to be at this show, and kept dancing around her stall, screaming at everyone. I tried to talk to her, but I couldn't get any words in between all her yelling, so I stopped.

After forever, Bubba came back. "How was it? Was it fun? Did you win? You look very shiny."

"I don't know if I won or not," he said. "But I did the course very well and if the judges do not make me the winner, they are wrong."

As he was getting unsaddled, MomToo came to my stall and brushed me, then put a saddle on my back. I looked around at it, and saw that it was not a shiny saddle with two pads and numbers. Even though I knew I was not going to show, I was a little sad. She put boots on my feet and wrapped my front legs, then she and Auntie Niki took me to the practice arena.

First, Auntie Niki longed me. I tried to gallop nicely and not buck and kick. There were lots of horses being longed, and I didn't want to crash into anyone. After I galloped and trotted, Auntie Niki put on my bridle and rode me around.

The other horses being ridden had funny saddles on. They were really little, and the riders all looked the same, with long boots on their feet and helmets on their heads. The horses had long legs and were stretching them out with each step, but they weren't going very fast. It was a much more relaxing arena than yesterday.

After Auntie Niki was done, she took me to MomToo. I was very happy when MomToo got into the saddle. Auntie Niki was telling her where to go and what to do. I tried really hard to listen and be a good horse. MomToo started out tense, but by the end of our ride, she felt relaxed and balanced. Most important, she felt happy.

I went back to my stall a happier horse. Maybe we would show next time.

After a few days, we got back in the moving box and went home. MomToo went back to riding me in the arena while Miss Tina told her what to do. We still had our good rides and bad rides. Even on the days when we had good rides, I could feel that MomToo thought she wasn't ready to go to a show. I didn't know how to change her feelings.

Soon, we went back to the Burbank place for another show. This time, I had been washed and banded, so I knew I would be in the arena with the judges. I was hoping MomToo would be riding me, but the first day it was only Miss Tina. MomToo wasn't even there to watch me. It was only Auntie Niki who saw me perform for the judges. Miss Tina and I went over the trail course well. Afterward, we walked back to the stalls, and Miss Tina tied me up next to the wheely-cart.

The wheely-cart is full of brushes and curries and boots and bottles of stuff I don't know about. Usually, they hang the long ropes from it, too. I was happy to be at a show, but a little sad that MomToo wasn't even there, much less showing me. The wheely-cart was so close, I thought I'd make the day more interesting, so I pushed it with my hip.

It fell over and everything spilled out of it. That made me happy. Just then, MomToo walked around the corner.

"I'm sorry I'm late," she said. "Traffic was awful."

"Do you see what your horse just did?" Miss Tina asked. "Didn't even startle him, either. He just knocked the cart over and looked at it."

"Maybe you shouldn't tie him that close," MomToo told her. "You know how he is."

"But I moved it out of his way."

"Not enough." MomToo was right. It was still in swinging range for me.

Auntie Niki didn't say anything. She was laughing.

MomToo and Auntie Niki straightened the wheely-cart and put everything back inside while Miss Tina took my saddle off.

"Well, he got a first and third in the green today," Miss Tina said. "Now that you're here, you can clean him up."

I went to the bath place with MomToo. I like the bath places at the shows, because they don't have cross-ties, so you can swing yourself left and right and play games with the water. MomToo doesn't seem to like them as much. I don't know why.

After a bit, she had my body rinsed and my tail washed, and we went back to my stall. Bubba was at the show with me again, so we talked about my being a first horse and a third horse, and then we got food.

The next day, MomToo was there to get me out with Auntie Niki. They longed me, then took me over to the trail arena. Auntie Niki rode me first, then MomToo rode me. Again, I tried to be a good horse for her and let her know that, if she could relax and stay balanced, we could be a team at the shows. She was happy when we were done.

It made me hope we would be in the show arena tomorrow, but when that day came, it was only Miss Tina who rode me. At least MomToo was there to watch. When Miss Tina and I did the course for the judges, I thought we did pretty good, except for one spot, where Miss Tina told me to lope around a turn that was really hard, then go over a pole that seemed like it didn't belong there. But I did my best, because we were a team.

"You know, you weren't supposed to go over that pole," Auntie Niki told us after we were done.

"I thought it was in a weird spot, but it looked like it was part of the wheel," Miss Tina said.

We went back to the barn, and MomToo took my saddle off, along with my extra tail, and the bands out of my mane. Bubba asked how I did, so I told him.

"Darn. That's a DQ," he said.

"What's a Dee-Cue?"

"I don't know what it means, except that you don't get any numbers called after your name. You're not even last. It's like you never did the course at all."

That sounded bad. Here I was, ending the show on a dee-cue. MomToo gave me an apple, anyway.

"You did good, Snoopy," she told me. "It's not your fault Tina took you over the wrong pole."

Maybe not, but it still didn't make me feel good.

CHAPTER FIFTY-ONE

The next day, we went back home. MomToo had a good ride on me at the show, so I expected her to come more to ride me, to get ready for the next show. Instead, she came less. Miss Tina rode me less, too, and Auntie Niki rode me more.

At first, I was worried. I thought they were mad at me for dee-cueing at the show. Maybe I should have known better. I asked Bubba if he knows where he's supposed to go on a course.

"Sometimes I have an idea, especially if it's the same course we've been practicing. But even if I do think I know, I wait for Miz Cee to tell me. That's what makes us a good team."

"So the dee-cue wasn't my fault?"

"Not unless your rider tells you to go somewhere and you ignore them and go somewhere else. Did that happen?"

"No. I went exactly where Miss Tina told me to go. It was really hard to get to, too."

"Then it was not your fault."

I was so frustrated, I blurted out, "I don't understand why I'm not being ridden more."

Bubba nickered to calm me. "That's not your fault, either. I heard the humans talking. Tina's grandson is very ill. Every day she makes plans to ride, and every day, something happens and she has to run to the hospital, or to help her daughter. Niki is taking care of us for her, but it is hard when she thinks she is doing one thing, and she ends up doing another thing instead."

"But what about my owner?"

"That I can't say, but I might guess that if her lessons are scheduled with Tina, they are having a hard time getting together."

"How are we supposed to get ready for the next show?"

"I do not know, but right now, it doesn't look like there will be a lot of horse shows if Tina's grandson does not get better."

I tried to understand why a human I did not know could keep me and MomToo from training and going to shows. If Miss Tina couldn't be there, I thought Auntie Niki could. She usually gave MomToo her lessons when we were at the shows anyway.

But over the days and days and days, it was just me and Auntie Niki. MomToo came to the ranch a lot. She gave me treats, and got me out of my stall and brushed me and let me run around the wood pen by myself. But she rode me so seldom, I barely remembered from one time to the next.

Every time she rode, I thought it might be our last time. I could feel her heart leaving me, and it made me sad.

CHAPTER FIFTY-TWO

On those few times that Miss Tina still rode me, she started doing things differently. She taught me that if she closed both legs around me, I was supposed to stop. Before that, I stopped whenever I heard the word *ho* and moved forward when I felt pressure on my sides. Now, I had to wait until I felt a soft tap against my sides to move, and if they were pressed firmly, I was to stop.

Once Miss Tina started teaching me that, Auntie Niki started doing it, too. The next time MomToo rode, she was surprised.

"Everyone's using a spur stop on their horses, so I decided to put one on your horse," Miss Tina told her.

MomToo seemed unhappy about this. "Why?"

"It just looks better."

MomToo rode me around that day, trying to stop me with her legs, but she was kind of bad at it. Either she got too much leg into me, or not enough. It didn't help that it was pretty new to me, too.

The good thing was we were more of a team. The bad thing was we were the kind of team that didn't know what we were doing. It would have been better to be a team that was helpful to each other.

After the spur stop, Miss Tina taught me that if she kept squeezing my sides, I was to walk backward. Of course, when she did that, Auntie Niki rode me that way, too. MomToo was even more surprised and unhappy after that was taught.

"You told me you wouldn't put a spur back on him," she told Miss Tina.

"I never said that. A spur back is part of a spur stop."

I'm a happy horse, in general. Sometimes I'm sad, or worried about things, but I usually see the good in whatever happens. So when I say that MomToo's ride that day was awful, I mean I don't remember her ever riding as badly. It was so bad, I felt sad until dinner came to cheer me up.

MomToo was right. She was never going to ride me in a show. And if she couldn't ride me in a show, how could I be useful to her? And if I wasn't a useful horse, how could I go to the Clover Fields when I die?

It was enough to keep me awake most of the night. When I did sleep, I dreamed of strange humans taking me from my stall, humans without any faces, taking me to a new stall where I didn't know anyone, and couldn't understand what my strange riders wanted.

"He's useless," one of them said. "Time for the teal truck."

I had to find a way to let MomToo know I was a good horse. My leg was healed. I was ready for her to show me. She just needed help to find a relaxed, balanced way to ride me so we could be a team, like Bubba and his owner.

One morning, MomToo came for her lesson. She got me ready and took me to the arena. This day, Auntie Niki was telling her where to go and what to do. I could feel MomToo try to do what Auntie Niki said, but her commands to me weren't very clear or firm. It felt like her heart was heavy and she wasn't trying to learn anymore. She waited for Auntie Niki to tell her what to do before she did it. I didn't think it was an awful ride, but it wasn't our best.

At the end, MomToo led me back to the cross-ties. I could tell she was unhappy. It felt like she was a jumble of darkness. Then I heard her say something to Auntie Niki that frightened me.

"I'm so unhappy right now. I feel like I don't know how to ride my horse anymore. You've all put new cues on him. I can't even hold my reins the way I used to. I just want to sell him and stop doing this. I feel like he's not my horse." Then MomToo let the water run out of her eyes from the sadness in her body.

Yes, MomToo, I told her. *I am your horse. I'll always be your horse. Don't sell me. Don't make me leave you and Mom and Bubba and my home.*

Of course, she didn't hear me, but maybe Auntie Niki did. She took my reins.

"I don't want you to be sad," she told MomToo. "Let's go down to the arena."

Auntie Niki led me back to the arena, then got in my saddle. MomToo followed. I felt a tap-tap on my sides and moved forward. Auntie Niki was talking the whole time.

"All we want to do is help Snoopy keep his head down. You don't need to shove your legs into him for a stop…" I felt a steady pressure, so I stopped. "…You just turn your toes out so that your spurs wrap around him… you can still say 'ho' if you want. There's no rule against it."

Then I felt a continued squeeze, so I walked backward. "The spur back is to keep his head level at the backup. Again, it's not shoving your leg in and pushing. It's just a steady pressure." She stopped pressing and I stopped backing, then she pulled on my reins, so I backed up. "See how his head lifts if I use the reins? Using our legs means he doesn't feel the pull on his face and doesn't bring his neck up."

She kept walking me, stopping, and backing, always talking to MomToo.

"It also helps, when you're backing him, to cluck to him. Nice and slow, at the pace you'd like him to back up." Auntie Niki clucked to me as she pressed on my sides and I backed.

"So, how do I make him go forward if I'm used to pressure to make him go?" MomToo asked.

"Fan him with your legs to get him started. Once he's moving forward, you can use your legs just like you usually do to make him go. It's when you sit back and wrap your legs that he stops."

They talked a little bit more, until Auntie Niki asked if MomToo felt better about the new commands and she said yes. Then MomToo led me back up to the cross-ties and unsaddled me. I wasn't sure if she was exactly happy, but she wasn't as sad as she had been.

CHAPTER FIFTY-THREE

MomToo was back the next day for another lesson. I was surprised that we didn't go over any poles. Auntie Niki kept telling her things, then she would stop me and they would talk about what Auntie Niki had said. We spent most of the time doing circles and turns. I could feel MomToo pushing my ribs over so that my shoulders were straight. We jogged and loped down the rail, then made circles. Auntie Niki kept telling her things, then saying, "Good. That's right. Good."

By the end of the lesson, I was jogging and loping with my shoulders straight and my hips pushing, just like with Auntie Niki. I could feel MomToo's balance really well, and turned every time she pushed into one side or the other. Her hand stayed quiet, and I even felt her sink into my back when her legs wrapped into my sides, so I stopped.

It was a good, quiet, relaxing lesson. MomToo was happier.

At our next lesson, we did the same thing as before, only we added poles. MomToo learned how to make sure my body was in the right place to go over the poles, and to guide me using the soft part of her leg. She also learned to kiss as I loped over a pole, if I needed to take a bigger step.

This was so different from our lessons before, when she would point me at the poles and ask for the walk, jog, or lope. Now she was actually making me use my body and steering me to the exact place on the poles. Sometimes, she forgot and got tense, and sometimes I couldn't quite figure out where her balance was, but most of the time, we did the poles the way we both liked to do them—the right poles at the right place, in the right gait.

MomToo was even happier after that lesson.

Soon, MomToo was riding a lot. Auntie Niki still rode me sometimes, too, and she was always in the arena, telling MomToo and I where to go and what to do.

I think MomToo was listening real well. She made sure I had walked, jogged, and loped with my body in the right place before we went over any poles. When she was happy with my body, we would start our trail work. She tried hard to let me know where she wanted me to go. If she wasn't clear, she learned to pick up the reins and make certain I understood.

The days started getting short, and the wind colder. It wasn't raining yet, but I knew it would start soon. This made me sad. MomToo and I were doing so well. I wanted to keep doing well so that she could show me. If the rains came, she wouldn't be able to ride because the arena would be too muddy. All of her happy confidence might leave.

One day, after our ride, MomToo took me to the wash rack and gave me a big bath. It had been almost forever since I had such a scrubby bath, and it felt good. After that, she put me in the cross-ties instead of on the hot walker to dry. Usually, she only did this if there were horses walking on the hot walker. Today she said something about keeping my legs clean.

The sun felt good on my body as I stood, drying. Soon, Bubba was next to me. He had a bath, too.

"I guess they thought we were dirty," I said.

"Maybe, but I got a bath because I'm going to a show."

That made me excited. I wondered if I was going to a show, too. Auntie Niki led me into the barn and gave me my answer. I was clipped, including my ears and legs. It was show time.

After my mane was banded, MomToo put my sleazie on, then my thin blanket, and put me back in my stall. "Don't mess up your mane," she said. "You're going to a show tomorrow."

I was very happy the next morning to see Miz Cee and Auntie Niki. They put Bubba and me and Gracie in Miz Cee's moving box.

Then we started going. The trees went sideways and the floor went up and down for a bit. It wasn't a long way. I didn't even finish my food.

When I got out, I was in an open area of dirt and weeds. There were empty stalls to my right, and arenas to my left. MomToo put boots and wraps on me, then the long rope. She picked up a whip and we walked toward one of the arenas. It felt so good to be at a show, I wanted to run and buck and scream, but I didn't. I promised myself to show MomToo I can be a good horse for her. So I just galloped, always staying at the end of the long rope and not pulling.

Auntie Niki watched us go around, telling MomToo to do things like reverse me or make me trot. I did everything she asked, until I was tired and she took me back to the moving box. I was tied to the side, and MomToo took my boots and wraps off, then brushed me. She and Auntie Niki put on my extra tail, then put two pads and the shiny saddle on. I looked back and saw numbers.

I was a little confused. "Bubba, why aren't we in stalls?"

"This is a one-day show. We haul in for the day, then go home."

"What am I supposed to do tied to the moving box?"

"Nothing, Snoopy. Eat your hay and wait to go into the show arena."

I waited, with my hay bag in front of me, for almost forever. Finally, Auntie Niki came around the trailer. Auntie Niki was wearing a big hat, like the judges wear. Usually Miss Tina wears one, too, when she rides me in the show arena. Since Miss Tina wasn't here, I thought Auntie Niki would ride me.

Then I saw MomToo. She also had a big hat on. She looked very shiny. I wondered if this meant she was going to show me. I had hoped this would happen for such a long time. I wanted to get excited about it, but I wasn't sure. I watched her look at a piece of paper. It was a trail pattern. At one point, I saw her look up and wave her finger around like she was tracing it in the air. I didn't know if she was really going to ride, or if she was just hoping to.

All of us walked up to the show arena, including Bubba and Miz Cee, and Gracie and her owner. I stood with MomToo for forever, while Auntie Niki rode Gracie and talked to her owner. Finally, Auntie Niki came over to us and got into my saddle. We rode around in the practice area, until she was happy with my body, and happy with me going over poles. Then we went into the show arena.

There was only one man with a hat today. He nodded and Auntie Niki rode me over the course. None of it was hard. I did harder stuff at home. It was actually so easy, I could have looked around, but I knew Auntie Niki would spank me if I did. Anyway, I needed to be a good and useful horse today for everyone.

We finished the course and left, so another horse could come in. Auntie Niki got off, and helped MomToo onto my saddle. We went to the practice area. Again, I went around, this time with MomToo, picking up my shoulders and pushing my hips forward as I loped and trotted poles. We did the gate together, and tried a backup. After a bit, Auntie Niki was happy with us and we went over toward the judge.

It was real. MomToo was going to show me.

CHAPTER FIFTY-FOUR

I thought of Uncle Snowy telling me to be a good horse and get back in the show arena. I thought about Bubba telling me about confident riders. I even thought of Kid Galahad and his belief that only good and useful horses go to the Clover Fields.

I wasn't certain if that was true, but today I could prove to MomToo that I was good and useful, and help her be confident. We walked into the arena and took our place by the first thing, the gate. I saw the judge nod at us, and felt MomToo reach for the gate's rope.

Right away, something felt weird. MomToo lifted up and out of my saddle, but I stayed where I was. She murmured some bad words about having short arms, but finally, she sat down and asked me to back up, from her spurs. I did as she asked.

We walked through the gate and she hung up the rope. She tapped my sides and I walked very straight. I felt her sit very balanced and put her right leg on me, so I started to lope. We loped around a wheel of poles to the left, then jogged right-left-right, then loped another wheel of poles to the right. Down to the jog again, we went through a box, turned sharp to the left, and into a chute. I had done all this with Auntie Niki. Now we were supposed to back around an L-shape.

I was so happy to have MomToo doing this, I'm afraid I got a little excited, and wanted to show her what a good horse I was.

Before she asked, I started backing up and turning around the corner. I didn't hit anything, but I was a little sloppy with my feet, and I felt her legs tap on me to get my attention.

"Wait for me, Snoopy," I heard her whisper.

We walked forward, turned a quick pivot right, and walked out over two poles that made an *X*. MomToo's balance was not quite in the middle of the *X* and her hand was a little jerky, but I knew what she wanted and made sure to step out over the middle.

And just that fast, it was done. MomToo had shown me for the first time. Auntie Niki came over and helped her off my saddle, then they hugged and Auntie Niki said, "Congratulations, you showed your horse."

Then they talked about the whole trail course and what was good and what was bad and they agreed it was bad for me to back up on my own and next time MomToo should stop me and make me slow down and listen.

Next time. They talked about a next time, like this would happen again.

I wanted to gallop to Bubba and tell him all about it. If the day I broke my leg was my saddest day ever, this was my happiest.

We walked back to the moving box and MomToo tied me up and left me alone with my hay. Bubba was still at the trail course. After a bit, MomToo came back. Her big hat was gone, and she didn't look so shiny anymore. She unsaddled me, then took out my bands and the extra tail.

"You were a good horse today, Snoopy. It was fun to be in the show with you. We're going to do this again."

My spirits lifted. She didn't need a better horse. She needed me. I stood very quiet and let her pet me without trying to reach out and grab anything. It felt nice.

While I stood there, Bubba came back.

"She showed me, Bubba," I told him. "My owner and I performed for the judge."

"And how did you do?"

I told him all about the course.

"Well, you could have let her back you around the corner, but for your first time together, it sounds like you did very well."

"I didn't hear my name and a number."

"That's because this is an all-day open-card show, so they are waiting until all the trail entries have gone before they figure out who won each class." He took a bite of hay, then said, "But no matter what, it sounds like you and your owner are finally a team."

I nodded. MomToo and I could only get better. We were a team.

CHAPTER FIFTY-FIVE

I found out later that I had been first horse with MomToo, which made her very happy. We went to one more show that year. I was a second and third horse that time. I kept waiting for us to go to another show, but we didn't. I was kind of sad that we didn't go to as many shows as when I was younger.

MomToo kept coming every week and riding me, while Auntie Niki told her what to do. Some days I felt lazy and made her work harder and some days I did what she asked the first time she asked me, but all our days together were good days. I missed the shows, but after a while, it was okay. We were happy.

Then one day I heard MomToo talking to Auntie Niki and Miss Tina about me.

"He's not the same horse as when he was three. He's got plates and screws in that leg and a fused joint. It makes him use his body in a different way. I want him to stay as sound and comfortable as he can for as long as possible."

"Well, of course," Miss Tina told her.

"So we're not going to campaign him. I don't want to overwork him and wear him out early. I like going to the shows and just having fun, but I don't want to take him to every show and try to qualify for the World. If we win, that's great. If we don't, I'm still having a good time. Going to the World is not a goal for me anymore. If we get there, it'll just be a perk."

I expected MomToo to be sad about not going to a lot of shows, but her heart felt very light, which made me happy. I guess I didn't have to worry whether I was a good enough show horse for her. She cared more about my leg, cared more about me, than she cared about showing.

I finally understood what Valentino had told me back at the hospital such a long time ago. I was blessed.

Me and MomToo at the Del Mar Nationals. We won!
(Photo by Rick Osteen Photography.)

EPILOGUE

Since then, MomToo has ridden me in every horse show I've gone to. Sometimes we are really good, and sometimes we are only partly good, but we're never plain awful. Now we are a team. It only took us eight years.

Bubba is still my friend. We are in the same barn and go to the same shows. He complains that he is getting older, and is not as good at trail as he used to be, but he is so handsome, he is used as a model for horse catalogs and magazines. And he's still spectacular.

Mom lives outside now. She is a lesson horse, like Wendy, which is a hard job, but she loves it because MomToo asked her to do it. She likes pleasing MomToo as much as I do.

Wendy is still teaching as well. She is a very old horse, but she still likes to teach students and is not ready to retire yet.

I will always miss Uncle Snowy, and try every day to remember his lessons.

The rest of my friends have either moved away, or gone to the Clover Fields. I miss them, too. I have new friends, but I still look for Holly or Uncle Snowy to show up in a new body. I even hope Kid Galahad surprises me someday.

When I was just a colt, my mother called me a simpleton and a brand new spirit. I've decided that must be a good thing, because I won lots of horse shows and made MomToo happy. Breaking a leg sure changes a guy, but I hope I'm still a simpleton. I'd like to make her happy until my spirit decides it's time to go eat clover.

THE END.
(Photo by Lynne Glazer Imagery.)

ABOUT THE AUTHOR(S)

Snoopy (aka One Flashy Investment) is a California boy who loves to throw things so much, he'd have been a major league baseball pitcher if he only had opposable thumbs. He was happy to dictate his story to his writing partner, equine patron, and MomToo, Gayle Carline.

Gayle gives her first horse Frostie all the credit for her writing career. She told her husband, Dale, that she wanted to write, so in 1999 he bought her a laptop for Christmas. A year after that, he gave her horseback riding lessons. When she bought Frostie, she finally started writing.

These days, she divides her days between writing humor columns for her local newspaper, writing mysteries for a larger audience, and spending quality time with her family: husband Dale, son Marcus, and four-legged kids Katy the cat, Duffy and Lady Spazzleton the dogs, and of course, Frostie and Snoopy.

For more merriment, visit her at http://gaylecarline.com, and be sure to check out Snoopy's blog at **http://thatsmysnoopy.blogspot.com**.

(Photo by Lynne Glazer Imagery.)

Made in the USA
San Bernardino, CA
17 September 2015